Henry Glemham

George Hern

A novel. Part 2

Henry Glemham

George Hern
A novel. Part 2

ISBN/EAN: 9783337065737

Printed in Europe, USA, Canada, Australia, Japan

Cover: Foto ©Andreas Hilbeck / pixelio.de

More available books at **www.hansebooks.com**

GEORGE HERN.

A Novel.

BY

HENRY GLEMHAM.

IN THREE VOLUMES.

VOL. II.

London:

SAMUEL TINSLEY & CO.,

10, SOUTHAMPTON STREET, STRAND.

1878.

GEORGE HERN.

CHAPTER I.

GEORGE HERN sat down to tea alone, not waiting, as usual, some half-hour for his father; for the delay caused by his gossip in the grove had already stirred up wrath within Mrs. Swindell.

Boulder, necessarily irregular in his comings and goings, did not reach Sunrise Cottage till nine o'clock, when it was fragrant with the scent of warmed-up mutton-slices and onions.

As soon as his father entered the sitting-room, George closed the law-book with which he had laboriously beguiled such part of his lonely evening as he had not devoted to his thoughts, and handed the fisherman his list slippers.

George Boulder, a worthy representative, in appearance, of the east-coast seamen, was as brown as an Egyptian, six feet two in height, and of mighty breadth, with rounded shoulders, lusty limbs, and not inactive movements. His features were large, but shapely. His grey eyes had a look of what I must term effrontery in them—it might have been called imperiousness, had he been of high degree—and could flash and sparkle under their bushy brows. His grizzled hair was long and strong, and mingled with the matted whiskers on each cheek. His upper lip was shaved, but he had a long beard, once as black as any Persian's, which, without being able to boast a curl, turned up at end as stubbornly as a Kahau monkey's.

He had a plain ring in each ear, and wore

a plaid scarf instead of a collar. For the rest, he had high sea-boots, a "sou'-wester'" hat, and a loose brown oil-slop, not fitting very advantageously.

Before the new-comer had tugged and shaken off his boots—no light task—Miss Swindell appeared at the door, and invited him and his son to join her parents at supper.

" It's almost the last night of my holidays, you know," she said, rather frigidly, and without looking at George ; " and my uncle Bilge is here, and can stay supper."

Boulder was hungry, and as his own store could produce cold meat only, and the scent from below was not unpleasant, the friendly invitation was accepted. So the fisherman exchanged his slop for a rough blue coat and a waistcoat made of monkey's skin, which he had purchased, years ago, from a Papuan in New Guinea, and went downstairs with his son.

Mr. Swindell had, of late, treated his lodgers with some little civility, for his wife had informed him of Rebecca's liking for young Hern, and he thought it worthy of timely encouragement. But the present act of hospitality emanated rather from the growing jealousy of the gardener's daughter, who had seen George Hern come from the grove, and had waited at her watching-place long enough to note that Miss Ashbocking followed him. She would draw some information from this young upstart this evening.

Mr. Bayard Swindell, formerly the admirer and, in a small way, the imitator of Cribb, Pearce, Belcher and the poetic Gregson, was a little above the middle height, broad of chest, but, as the folds of his clothes would tell you, thin of limb—a wiry, bony man. He had a pear-shaped head, a stern eye, a large well-formed nose, but a mouth devoid of beauty and resembling a frog's. Not, as Mr. Oscar Ashbocking once remarked, that this point of resemblance brought him at all into that contempt which Swedenborg seems to think the frog deserves; for Mr. Swindell was considered, among the simple, a man of some mark. He was upright in his gait, and had something of a bullying and official air, traceable partly to his old pugilistic habits and partly to his pride in his present appointments of verger (commonly called dog-rapper) in the church and a special constable of the borough. He had, like most of the notabilities of Heathhammock, a nickname—" Bumper," in allusion to his bumptious demeanour. He was also sometimes called " Cut-away ;" but I cannot correctly account for the origin of this title. Some say it was suggested by his one short fist-conflict with Boulder, which ended in his retreating and crying for quarter ; others by his activity in the use of his knife at meals.

Perhaps his most conspicuous articles of dress were his blucher-boots and coarse grey socks, to which the shortness of his corduroys seemed to invite attention.

Mrs. Swindell was a fat, but pale and sour-looking person, some years older than her husband, and who, like Philematium, had disguised her age when she married him.

Her dress seemed to indicate that she had some of the propensities of the class known as "the shabby genteel," or, in Heathham-mock phraseology, "the dirty fine;" but she had been too well schooled as a servant in good families to neglect her house, which was always tidy and clean.

Rebecca Swindell was a large, "bouncing" young woman, with a round face, strangely like a cat's, bright large eyes, a short nose, not ugly, but very unlike her father's, and great coils of hair piled high upon her head, and fixed in their place by a comb of some pretensions. Her rich-coloured lips moved rather restlessly, but the voice of this substantial person was feeble and shrill.

As to her garb, it would draw no severe criticism, perhaps, from the friends she would meet during her holidays ; but, at Bayswater, she was considered a persistent and irreclaimable "ill-dresser," and was once sarcastically alluded to as having been created for the serviceable purpose of warning others against the neglect of taste in dress.

The remaining partaker of the mutton and onions was Mr. Bilge, the butler of Castle House, whose beaming smiles made his face a contrast to his sister's in expression, though it resembled it in breadth.

"You must take us as we are, neighbour,"

said Mr. Swindell, in a mild voice; for, in
the presence of his wife, especially when sup-
plemented by that of his daughter, the hec-
toring airs of this man of office usually faded
(to quote Boulder) "like a red rag dropped
into the oven."

"An' a very good take too, mate," said
Boulder.

"To be sure," said Bilge, with his smile.
"It might not suit the Admiral——"

Here he paused, for he was cautious in the
indulgence of his tendency to backsliding
insinuations in the presence of George Hern.

"It's easy for you to talk about supper, an'
to guzzle it, Swindell," said the gardener's
wife; "but the gettin' of it ready is another
thing, and it's a cryin' shame that men don't
think no more o' that."

"I do think of it, my dear," said Mr. Swindell. "But, now, only yesterday I was
talkin' with Mrs. Pittock's coachman, an' he

was grumblin' at his mistress's new harness, which, for all it's nice looks, is terrible stiff i' the buckles, he says; 'but what do the women think about that?' says he."

"You've been very quiet this evening, Mr. George," said Rebecca, looking with assumed indifference at Hern; "I wonder you don't ruin your eyes reading so much, after being shut up in the office all day."

"My examinations make a good deal of reading necessary," said George.

"There's no good done i' this world without hard work," said Boulder; "an' George has bin i' the right all along to go about his business body and soul, leavin' none of his wheels unturned nor yet ungreased; workin' double tides, goin' at it like a road-mender to a heap o' frosted stones. No hesitatin' in duty. I'm an arnest man. I'm for strict discipline. Though a rover, I've been a man-o'-war's-man in my time."

" Isn't the law rather dull, Mr. George ?"
said Rebecca.

" Devil take the dulness," cried Boulder.
" I beg pardon for that word—but don't tell
me o' the dulness o' the law ! It's sound
and steady ; an' it's better 'an louder soundin'
schemes; better 'an all the talk about pro-
spectin' mighty fields salted wi' diamonds
—and that like."

" You're right, Mr. Boulder. There's
nothin' like steady work, as I tell Swindell,"
said the gardener's wife, who waged incessant
war upon her husband's predilection for
leisure and for occasional visits to the
Lug-sail Inn.

" You've found · that out, ma'am," said
Boulder. " If you hadn't bin' a steady
worker, you'd never ha' bin so well re-
membered in Lady Pidgeon's will. There
was your father, Pilot Bilge, now ; he never
did any good for himself."

This remark did not please Mrs. Swindell, who was rather proud of her father, the Trinity Pilot, and was not fond of reference to her days of service—when she was called "Ann," though her name, as her old sampler and the Heathhammock register would prove, was "Jerusha."

"My father has left a good name behind him," said Mrs. Swindell; "an' besides, no one need to think that I haven't had no relations who knew how to make money. I'd an aunt, who was a mill-stone balancer's widder down in the north, who'd lots of housen an' cottages, an' should ha' left me something, which she always hinted like she'd do it. But the money went away, an' she lived an' lived into such a poor bedraggled thing an' didn't die peaceful."

If the speaker had gazed at her husband's face through the steam from the dish before him, she would have seen some signs of satisfaction upon it, as he thought of the good sum safely secured from Lady Pidgeon. He had put up with a good deal for the sake of that money.

" I can't help thinking you do more work than other people try to do, Mr. George," Rebecca resumed ; " I expect you're rather ambitious."

" Some folks are too fond o' work, and others ain't fond enough," said Mrs. Swindell, with a hard look at her husband. " And some folks go dawdlin' on from day to day without a hap'orth of ambition."

" You'd better out with it, missis, if you've anythink to say," said the gardener; "but I wish you'd let me be at peace in my home. Haven't I enough to bear at my work, some-times—not from the weight o' the work itself, so much——"

" I should say not," said Mrs. Swindell, drily.

" But from some o' the folks. There's
Mrs. Oscar (no disrespect, Mr. George)—
no man nor yet angel can call her a gardener's friend, for she don't give you no
encouragement. A rose is a fool to her
compared with a red cabbage ; and a sh'lott
suit her a sight better than forty pickeltees,
which please on'y the two top storeys, as I
may say, or the genteel part o' the face,
eyes and nose. She look out for the mouth,
which lead down into the lower premises.
She was casting her looks, rather hungry-
like, the other day, at some o' the old trees ;
but I don't think Miss Clara nor yet the
master wouldn't stand to that. I shouldn't
wunner if the misses 'ud like to hev 'em cut
down and turned into money, and the place
made like a bit o' copperho'd land, where
there's nayther tree, nor beech, nor bit of
oak about it."

" Do you think Miss Clara is very fond

of the garden and the grove, Mr. George?" asked Rebecca, busily buttering a rusk.

George looked at her narrowly. Clara's allusion to the report this maiden had set on foot about him had been present to his mind all the evening; and it now suddenly occurred to him that she might have strengthened her opinion by the discovery of his visit to the grove. The thought did not greatly disturb him, for Clara's revelations had taken away all hope of his love-compact remaining long a secret.

"I think so," he answered drily, for he was little inclined to enter upon the sacred subject to which he thought she was trying to lead him.

"You're right, she is," said Mr. Swindell; "and so's the master, in his way. But, by Joseph, his talk, which it might fit you, Mr. George, ain't the thing for me, though handy when you get into a scrape," he muttered, in allusion to the interview mentioned by Admiral Howsegoe to his grandson.

" He has two sentences ready for you when you next meet him, Mr. Swindell," said George ; " a quotation from a Dr. Coachi as to the origin of the word ' bumper,' and a passage about one Papirius, who brought two kinds of apple-trees from Syria and Africa to Italy. But we won't talk of our betters behind their backs."

" Betters in point o' money, Mr. George," said Bilge, with a cunning look at his niece.

" Well, Mrs. Oscar has the knack o' treatin' folks as if she was their better," said Mrs. Swindell. " There's a little too much of the tyran' about her for my likin'."

" So there is for mine ; though, perhaps, I ought not to say it, Mr. George," said Bilge. " But, really, it's tryin' to have her interferin' at our house ; an', though she can't abide the Admiral, she will look after him at meals, just for the sake o' finding fault with our missis an' our ways. 'The salt to the Admiral;' 'the Admiral will take some bread'—that's her manner o' doin'."

"She's got too much o' the tyran', as I said," repeated Mrs. Swindell; "an' that's a thing I can't abide."

"And yet you try to make me like a dog with his tail cut off," thought Mr. Swindell. But he said aloud,—"Certainly that poor Trippinton is worrited into bein' a soft-head, and no mistake; glidin' an' slidin' about, as if afraid o' makin' any mortial sound."

"She's a poor ticket," said Boulder, "an' sometimes seem, as you may say, to be a'most apologizin' for her existence. But George say she's partial to her mistress. An', as he say also, don't let's talk about our betters here."

"But do you like Mrs. Oscar yourself, Mr. George?" Rebecca interposed, before another subject was commenced.

" There's much to like in her," was his reply.

" Is she nice sometimes ?" Rebecca added.

" She can be nice enough," said her interfering father ; " just as she can 'commodate her craw to be nice enough accordin' to her place. At home, plain food ; at other folks' expense, all the dainties she can lay hand on."

Mrs. Swindell was annoyed to hear her daughter's course of examination, to which she was privy, thus foiled by interruptions from another tongue than her own.

" You're in a chatterin' humour, Swindell," she said, sharply.

" What matter for that, if I've somethin' to chatter about, my dear ?" said the gardener, benignly.

" I ain't so sure about your matter," she retorted.

" What !" he exclaimed, in an injured

rather than a self-asserting tone. " I don't pass for a ninny out of my own home. Am I a man to take a blackberry for a blue-bell, or hops for a bargain o' cornflowers, or a pea-sheaf for a lapfull of oat-grass an' ill weeds that perish ? Ain't this here hid o' mine no better an' a bee-hive ? Ain't these here eyes no brighter nor more meanin' 'an a laurel leaf, an' ain't this here mouth a man's ?"

" It take enough food into it to feed a herd o' hogs," said his wife ; "an' as to drink——"

" Pray, mother, let us keep from that subject," said Rebecca, anticipating a tedious interchange of recriminations and excuses.

" I must have my glass, now and then," said the gardener, a little ruffled by his wife's discourteous interruption of his eloquence. " It's my natur', an' you can't bind a man with rules an' words agin his natur'. But, as Becky says, let's say no more about it."

" Here's Mr. Boulder, to teach you how to

be moderate," said Mrs. Swindell, accustomed
to have the last word; "an' that's all I ask
of you."

"Ay, be moderate, mate," said Boulder,
"in your drink, and in your talk too.
Too much of a good thing spoil all. A
man wouldn't care to hev a hunderd larks
all singing close to his ear at the same
time. And, as to drink, a man had better go counting wheat-stalks or bulrushes
with an empty stomach, than sit soakin' in
a publichouse, especially if he hev a wife
which don't fancy such ways; for if a man
put the gentleness out of his wife, he'll find
it a hard job to know how to tackle her;
an' he'd better hev a shark, or a snake,
or a beastly-smellin' pole-cat to tackle,
which he'd know leastways how to get at
them!"

At this point Bilge rose to walk home, and
Rebecca, with a mortified aspect, followed

him a few steps from the house. She had already told him of her discovery.

" I could draw nothing out of him, you see," she said. " There were so many interruptions. But you must do what you can in the matter. You may depend upon it, unless Mr. Storker looks sharp he will fail."

" And be beaten by such a chap as that ?"

" He's a stuck-up chap, but there's something about him—not that I care an atom, you know. Good-night."

Immediately after Rebecca's return to the house, Boulder and his son ascended to their own room, where George undertook the customary duty of reading aloud a page of a time-worn book of family prayers, and afterwards joined his voice with his father's in singing the first and last verses of the evening hymn. This was a somewhat inharmonious performance, for the elder vocalist had not a musical ear, and his tones marred the charm of his son's. Mr. Swindell had once remarked that he would rather hear a lot of fire-irons knocked together. But the rough fisherman enjoyed and reverenced this nightly psalmody.

CHAPTER II.

SHORTLY after five o'clock on the following day, whilst Mr. Swindell was snoring in his bed, notwithstanding his wife's innumerable stern allusions to the advantages of early rising, George Hern was dressed and standing at his father's bedside.

" I should like to take a walk with you, if you can spare a little time before breakfast," he said. " I want to tell you something which I did not wish to mention last evening on the verge of your night's rest, for it might have spoiled it. I didn't improve my own by thinking of it."

" Lad, you mustn't lay awake o' nights

now your examination's drawin' on so near," said Boulder anxiously. " But I'll be ready for you," he added with his wonted impetuosity, " I've not had a good chat with you for a matter o' many days."

As they passed downstairs they heard Mrs. Swindell address her husband in rather thick tones : " There go them lodgers, lazy-bones, and you gruntin' here. I shall have to go to the old plan o' settin' the clock forward for you."

" Ugh !" muttered Boulder, "it's no business o' mine, but that's a rum way o' beginnin' the day. But they're nayther of 'em muchers, and there's no great shakes between 'em. I'd as lief be a sea-surgeon fish, as marry her."

George opened the back-door, startling from the dewy garden a large blackbird, who sent a loud note from his yellow beak as he sped over the wall towards Mr. Ashbocking's grove. Boulder then took his customary careful survey of the sky, and they marched down Silver Lane to the Common. They decided to walk to Yellow Point, the ferryboat landing-place, a little below the junction of Samphire Creek with the tawny Ant.

On the way George gave his father the gist of Clara Ashbocking's conversation of the preceding evening.

" Then it's all out, an' there's rocks ahid, lad," said the fisherman after listening with many suppressed ejaculations to his son's words.

" Of course I couldn't expect to escape this discovery long," said George.

" No, an' I've often hinted like (I've bin mighty secret over this matter, as you wished) that you might be goin' a knot too fast in tryin' after this lass, though a pretty bird, an' worth the winnin'. It might ha' bin' better," he added rather tartly, " to ha' bin content wi' gettin' to become, as you are, a gentleman an' well set i' the world, without a wife. Not but what I know the outsides an' middles o' you well enough to be sartin no grand wife 'ud make you any different to me. It ain't that. I know you'll stick to me, an' be a comfort to me, an' I sometimes think," he continued solemnly, " that your poor mother (God be with her, an' forgive me), if she can take any manner o' note of us, find it a comfort to see how we've been happy together, an' how you mean to stick to me, an' be good to me to the last."

" I hope, father, that my intention to do my duty faithfully to you won't perish amongst my many impracticable schemes. I've a very heavy debt to repay you, if I can."

" I've done what I could for you, lad, since the time when I led you by the hand, an' my great rough paw wasn't noways accustomed to such a tender little bunch o' fingers. It seem but a year or two since I used to laugh at your little bits o'clothes, an' now you're pretty near in the same tier as your master, an' as strong as a young whale, an' thinkin' o' marryin'! But beware o' women, George; they are as fond o' playin' fast an' loose as a sailor of a trip ashore."

" I've often made you warm and drawn a hard word or two from you by smiling at your advice," said George; "I know I am very apt to do so when you talk about women, for the one woman in whom I take an interest lies a little above the reach of your rules and warnings."

" Ay, ay !" said Boulder, shaking his head; " it's easy to smile. There's much I can't teach you, but there's much you've yet to learn. Young folks may think they can make sugar o' winkle-shells, an' build a derrick wi' their naked hands; but not a bit of it. They mustn't be saucy and conceited !"

" No, no," said George smiling ; " but don't blow me up now, father."

" I'm for no blowin'-up," said Boulder gloomily. " The word seem to hit me, lad. When a man make such big mistakes as I've made in my time, they seem to take away from him the privilege of judgin' and weighin' other folks' little faults and fools'-tricks. Put that in your mind. But give me all the respec' you can, for you'll grant I've bin a pretty good father to you, in spites o' the wrong-doin' at your birth, an' in spites o' the prison and my little slips aboard-ship here an' there, an' especially in regard o' the slave-trade."

" Which I was once going to oppose, indirectly, in another quarter," said George.

" Yes ; confound that warlike sperrit which you took from me (though the Herns ha' bin no doves) : it's done mischief enough a'ready. If you hadn't gone back to see them soldiers

at Raddison, I shouldn't ha' laid hands on
poor Bedinfiel'; an' I s'pose it's the same
sperrit as made me go in for him, an' like-
wise made me tackle the police at Liverpool,
which seemed to set the wardens o' the
prison there pretty strong agen me, I
thought. But I've bin a good father, on the
whole, to you."

" To be sure. I have a tremendous debt
to repay you. Your steadfast affection and
faithful sheltering care have been of great
service in giving me a fair opinion of the
world, which is not a small acknowledgment,
considering my silly sensibility and the only
stain on my birth, which might, in my young
days, have set my hand against every man
and every man's hand against me; and considering my close application since to the
duties of a lawyer, who 'but beholds the
baser side of life,' according to a poet of
whom it has been written that 'All phe-

nomena of Heaven and earth' he 'traced to their causes' by another poet, though the poetry of this latter has been very sharply stigmatised by a third. We were on this subject a few evenings ago in the study."

" I've done my duty by you, but let's hev no more o' the past," said the appeased fisherman. " You must make allowances for my temper, for I've been through a lot o' worritin' an' a lot o' trouble. As to the future, my pays hevn't come up to the mark I hoped for ; but I shall be a torrerble sum to-wards the lot we want, an' I think I can make a friend. An' as to the balance, as you've often said, there's no doubt as Mr. Ashbocking 'ill be glad to have you stay a time after that you are full-fledged, an' you can work out, without pay, what I hevn't made up at the time."

" No doubt this could be managed. I don't wish to boast, father, but I feel so convinced of my usefulness in the office that I'm quite sure they will miss me much if I leave."

" No doubt o' that," said Boulder, in a tone of satisfaction. " But I wish I could ha' scraped all the money together," he added rather dolefully, " I've tried my best."

" And have done much, have done nobly."

" I've been wunnerful careful o' my moneys, an' I might hev had wuss luck, an' p'r'aps I hevn't no right to complain. I sometimes think so, when I see a large heap o' fish, shinin' and silver-like, an' fleshy an' wholesome-lookin'. They make me feel thankful : for, after all, what a poor hand we men hev in the matter ! But, to be sure, there ain't much comfort in a great heap o' fish, an' a good stock o' lines and nets, an' lock dans, an' dan tows, an' anchors, if the prices o' fish ain't right, an' a man can't save on 'em, or if there's no manner o' prospec' of another good haul for a long time to come."

" There are pleasures as well as hardships in a fisherman's life," said George a little wistfully.

" Ay, ay; but you don't want to be botherin' your brains about fishermen an' the sea. You'll never want to know a sole from a flounder, nor a pilchard from a sprat. But, thank the Lord, I think you're settled ashore for good an' all now, moored stem and stern, so to speak, though not at sea, an' the rights of it too."

At this moment a white bull-terrier cantered past, and, on turning, they saw Storker Ashbocking walking about a hundred yards behind them, with the sluggish Ariel at his side.

" He carry a deal o' flesh an' weight now," said Boulder, in a surly voice. " He's a clumsy chap. They'd never go to shove you aside from the pretty bird for that bunglin' bum-boat of a chap; an' as to family ties,

they oughtn't to pay no more regards to them
than to so many yards o' cat-gut. If you've
only got that chap agin you, a little time 'ill
lay her ahold all right, for they might as well
show her a icy Greenlander or a thick-
skulled, full-blooded nigger, as such a lumber-
ing Englishman."

Storker gained upon Boulder and Hern,
and was soon walking beside them.

" I'm glad to see you two again," he said
cheerily.

"Same to you, sir," said Boulder with a
side-long and not very complimentary glance ;
" you're up early."

" I'm going over to Southaston to Job
Futter's. I saw him in Cliff Street last
night, and he told me he was crazed with
rats, and thought of putting some ferrets to
work this morning. I'm going to test my
foreign dog. Ariel followed us without invitation. He's welcome; but I hope he

won't cross Molock, so as to attract his teeth,
instead of a rat. I have to be at business
in good time this morning, so I have
tumbled out at this unearthly hour—a proceeding not very palatable to me. Why
Hern, you're looking well, neat, intellectual,
etc.; but there's not much of the pome-
granate's hue in your face. You have been
working hard, man. They tell me you're a
useful and rising man."

" An' I hope they tell you right, sir," said
Boulder ; " risin' as well as useful ; for a man
may be useful just as a mere hawspipe's
useful. Not but what a mere useful, honest
man 's to be set some store by, whether he
be, so to speak, o' the mizen-top, or the
main-top, or the fore-top. But George is
risin', and I thank God for it, though he do
tell me such things as not to drink my tea
out o' saucer, and not to call picturs
' gays.' "

"Well, Boulder," said Storker, "I think there is some credit due to you for getting our friend here to settle down so well. There used to be some dangerous fire in him; and as to his being cooped up all these years in an office, I often feel amazed at the fact, considering his strong love of liberty. I have heard Mr. Service say he would chafe like a maniac when he was taken captive at 'prisoners' base,' though he would run the greatest of risks."

"He's a very good sample o' the tamed wild spirit," said Boulder with a smile, "for he might ha' growed up like me; for I was like him as a boy or wuss, an' cared nothin' for a wettin' nor for darkness, for I'd as lief be out at nights as the cows. I'd drive a dozen pins into my thigh to the head for sixpence, and bend a pewter pot altogether out o' shape by pressin' it agin' my forrid. I can remember when I was dared to go into a grocer's stores, where the sugar and raisins were ; an' I got caught, an' they shut me up in a empty hogshid. But I'm a fool to talk o' these things. George is settled down an' quiet, sir : a fixtur', like the Floatin' Light with its mushroom anchors, only better, for he ain't on the sea at all."

" No, but he's near it. What a face you would wear if you discovered one morning that our friend had run away to sea in the night!"

" He'll never do that ! Anything but that ! I've begged of him, a'most on my knees, to do anything but that. Breath o' my body ! I was thinkin' on'y the other day what a tale the sea have told to folk we know since George have been at the law ! There was that poor Bob Burleigh killed by the bustin' superheater aboard the steam-ship *Ethelbert.* There was the *Suffolk Gal* come to grief, losin' I don't know what—starboard bulwarks to the taffrail riggin' rail, manisal, topyard, stanchions, jibboom an' head- stays. There was poor Chalker broke his leg fallin' off the mast, sailin' from Plymouth wi' pipe-clay. There was poor Horner on'y saved in the wreck o' the *Little Sue* wi' carger of onions, by hangin' on a hen-coop. An' there was Tom Spike and the three Browns went down i' the *Jonathan Twad- dells* when bound for Truro wi' carger of arsenic, when the snow was enough to smud- der a poly bear, and the gale reminded old folks o' the time when we had two an' forty craft ashore hereabouts for twenty mile o' coast."

" My father talks in the horrified tone of a land-lubber," said George, " yet he has faced the dangers of the sea year after year with the greatest deliberation—though he is very chary of telling me of his adventures."

" Where's the use ?" said Boulder hastily.

" I've got too much warm good-will for you.
I know something o' the meanin' o' pumps
choked, water-casks lost, jettison o' deck-
load an' carger, losin' anchor an' fifty fathom
o' chain, mainmast sprung, an' chain-plates
started. I've bin i' the Arabian Ocean an'
i' the Coral Sea, an' I have plucked Tahita
hog-plums from the tree. I've sailed amongst
the sandbanks o' the Cattegat, an' I've bin i'
the Firth o' Forth in a fog. I know somethin' o' the Arctic floes an' the miles o' pack-
ice, an' I've tasted the storms o' the Equinox
a, many times. But, as true as I walk on
this solid ground, I'd rather be pushed into
my grave afore my time than have this son
o' mine take to seafarin' or do as I've done."

" There's not much cause for fear on that
score now, I should say," said Storker. " He's
likely to become more familiar with the
screeching of the pen than with the roaring
of the gale."

"Ah! the roarin' o' the gale, an' the splinterin' o' the masts, an' the snappin' o' the ropes, an' the damnable spiteful sleets that cut you till you are stupefied and blue wi' the cold an' ready to howl. You'd better be shut in a caravan o' Rewshan wolves."

"You haven't given me much chance of getting a taste for rowing and sailing, father," said George.

"No," said Storker, "and I've often thought it rather hard lines. Here's a fellow who would have taken an oar in the lifeboat with a crushed finger——"

"I was right, I was right," said Boulder. "I was not goin' to make a sort o' half sailor o' the boy. A seafarin' man is the wust of seafarin' things for land purposes. Ship-wood is good for many things, and ship's stays make good wire-rope for palin's, but a seafarin' man ain't wuth so much as a tenter herrin'. Let wise folk stick ashore."

" Well, I confess I shouldn't care to be out at sea on a dirty night," said Storker; " I'd as willingly sleep in a tank with forty lizards, or be shut up ten years in the Eddystone."

" And the rights of it, too," said Boulder; "you'd better be a live eel next the lid in a crammed basket than go out to sea in dirty weather, unless forced."

"One ought to ride a jibbing horse to appreciate a steady one," said Storker, "and one ought to hear you talk about the sea to appreciate a life ashore. So you and I, George Hern, must settle down on *terra firma*, and be thankful."

" I'm told, sir," said Boulder, nudging his son slyly, "that you're thinkin' o' settlin' down in arnest with a wife an' all. Let an old man give you a little more advice, an' beware o' the women. As I told this boy a few minutes back, beware o' them."

" I most heartily agree that your warning

words are full of wisdom," said Storker readily, though his voice seemed to have lost some of the ring of scorn that used to characterise his criticisms of the gentle sex. " It's a monstrous pity we can't do without women with their blunderings, and fooleries, and narrow thoughts, and false surmises. Scurrying, precipitate simpletons, who can hardly grasp a moderately-important subject, but who will rush with intense eagerness after a paltry excitement, be it a circus procession, or a funeral, or a smartly-dressed toy-shop, or a cripple ! A squib suits them better than a comet."

" It *is* a pity we can't do without 'em," said Boulder, interposing to prevent a protest from his son against Storker's severe words ; " for there's few on 'em can 'arn their rations. My blessed stars ! think of a crew of 'em in downright dirty weather. Who'd like to be aboard ?"

"I'd rather be corked up in a gas-pipe," said Storker. "Think of a lot of nursery-maids in a square formed for cavalry."

"Ay," continued Boulder, again nudging his son, "an' these women are so conceited an' such puzzlers, wi' their twaddlin' an' their bibble-babblin', an' their flouncin', an' their fondlin', an' their sharpness, an' their simple-ness, they'll puzzle you. To think o' the words I've had with that there Mrs. Josham, who had half a mind to marry me. I reckon I have knowed that woman fifteen year off an' on, an' I hevn't summed her up yet, though I used to call on her pretty often when she was laid on the shelf wi' lumbago eighteen week, an' I paid a bit towards her doctor's bill, which made me timid o' treatin' myself to meat for two month (for I've been obliged to be careful o' my moneys)."

"It's unmanly on our part," said George, "to attack women in this way. I disagree entirely with you, Mr. Storker. In their gentle way women are very wise, as well as very good. I have heard Mr. Oscar say that, in his opinion, there are few wise men who have not found their wisdom almost doubled in real worth if they have lived some years with good wives."

" I think that the help of a good wife is confined for the most part to the making of slippers, the mending of shirts, the peeling of walnuts, and the shelling of shrimps," said Storker. " But I acknowledge, George Hern," he added, plucking two or three wavy-edged, heart-shaped leaves of wild sea-kale, and fixing them in his button-hole, " that there are women who are above and beyond my criticism. Good-morning, worthies. I shall see you shortly, Hern."

They had reached the ferry landing-place, and the father and son stood to watch their companion's passage across the river with his dogs. The tide was running rather sluggishly, and the bubbles in the water-wreaths around the piles of the landing-platform were feeble and few. Down from the harbour-mouth came the old sad murmur of the mighty sea, still quarrelling with the un-productive beach for utterly severing it from the more fruitful land (except where the pinched tidal rivers offer temporary outlets). A melancholy breeze swept across the common, its whisper broken at times by the pipings of a few golden plovers wheeling far overhead.

There was a depressing absence of signs of life around. The funnel of a little steam-ship, moored a short distance down the river, was purifying itself, in silence and loneliness, with such waves of salt air as might eddy down its black throat in their course ; and some lazily-swaying boats could be seen along the river banks. The few houses of

Southaston seemed invested with an air of drowsiness, as well as the church in its robe of ivy and framework of dull silver cloud.

" This place doesn't improve my spirits, father," said George Hern, turning from the river. " Let us go home, and think about the day's work."

" You shouldn't hev interfered when I was leading him on," said Boulder ; " sure-LY you saw my drift. I could ha' led him on to curse the whole o' the womankind, big an' little. I could drive this chap out o' the field altogether !"

The half-deadened cry of a cuckoo floated upon their ears from the woods of Mr. Bethell Ormerod, which stretched to the borders of Southaston. George quickened his pace, as he said, with a sad smile and a strangely anxious expression :

" Your line of conduct might hardly suit the circumstances, father. I won't infringe on the good and honest frankness that lies between us, but I think you must leave me to act for myself in this delicate and dangerous matter."

" George, lad," said Boulder, stopping with his hands on his son's shoulders, and looking into his face with a seriousness that was somewhat pathetic, " don't you speak to me in that tone an' don't you give me one sign o' your bein' likelys to give way an' fancy a lot o' new trouble ahid. I've bin through much. The queer sort o' feelin' o' these past few years, the goin' agin long habit which seemed my very nature like, hev put a strain on me which you can't figger to yourself; and, by Heaven, I can't tell what would happen to me if my great hopes was to be damaged much !"

CHAPTER III.

AFTER Storker had set out for the town-clerk's office, his grandfather and parents held a conclave at Castle House respecting him, the Admiral opening the proceedings by repeating the news given him by Bilge, when he brought his shaving-water that morning, as to Clara's interview with George Hern in the grove.

" Action must be taken at once !" exclaimed the Admiral in conclusion, his usually dull eyes brightening with excitement. "As I have often hinted to you, I have set my soul on this girl for Storker for a long time, but especially of late; and the Andreys and

Ormerods are cleared out of the way beauti-
fully. This marriage is the very thing ; and
I must, and will, have it carried out, in spite
of any such article as George Hern, or any
amount of paltry difficulties !" He then en-
larged upon the plans he had shadowed out
to Storker, ending with the weighty proposal
that Castle House should be appropriated to
the young couple.

"Give up Castle House directly!" cried
Mrs. Kidd, elevating her eyebrows spasmo-
dically. " I don't think Storker will wish to
treat his mother so !"

" You won't spoil my schemes by your
absurdity," said the Admiral, sharply. " The
sacrifice is necessary ; and, besides, I simply
propose that you should give place to another
Housegoe, as it were—your own son. And
you look very doubtful, mister," he added, in
a domineering tone, to Mr. Kidd. " You
may consider this a mere blundering notion,

but I have thought about these things hour
after hour, and my plan is right. The one
essential point is to please Mary Ann, and—
not to mince matters—to give her the idea
that we have plenty of money. What stroke
can be better than your coolly giving up this
house to her daughter ? It will be a splendid
bribe even for that ' Nipper.' Even now,
too, she is well inclined towards the match.
You can go into a quiet place, with little expense ; but, if you take a tolerable house for
the young people, you will have to lay out a
good sum to put it in such order as the exact-
ing Mary Ann will expect. I propose that
Kidd should keep on the banking business
for a little time after the marriage. If there
are any unpleasant signs in that quarter, they
had better be kept under a napkin till the
marriage makes us able to uncover everything. It might have been better for Kidd
to have consulted me as to his affairs many a

time before to-day; but to-day I come forward with advice, and I intend to worry you till it is carried out."

The banker drew a deep breath, looked anxiously at the Admiral, and took off his spectacles to wipe them.

" Well, Kidd ?" said Admiral Howsegoe.

" In regard to the bank, sir," said his son-in-law, nervously, "you seem to think it possible——"

" That there are signs of rottenness ! You and I will talk about that hereafter," said the Admiral, with a vigorous (but painful) motion of his head towards his daughter.

But she would not be thrust out of their discussion.

" Good gracious !" she exclaimed, looking mournfully from one to the other. " At last something dreadful has happened. I've never interfered, Kidd, but I've always had some doubts, especially in regard to the expensive curiosities, and the wasted time, and so on. What is the world coming to? I'm not likely to be a long liver, with the best of times; and now something dreadful has happened at the bank to shorten my days."

" Once for all, Arabella," said the Admiral, sternly, "you, gossip as you are, are to drop that subject; but remember that I tell you, in all earnestness, that it is of the utmost importance to your son's position that this marriage should be brought about if possible. And, once for all, Kidd, you must know that I have had, as I had a right to have, a few words in strict confidence with your Mr. Anguish, and that I have learnt that things are not so healthy at the bank as I could wish. But let there be no hint, no mention of this, outside this house until after Storker's marriage. This will set all right. Upon my honour, I am most anxious about this mar- riage, and I named these things to Storker yesterday. He can be brought round, I think. It may not be essential for you to leave Castle House, of course; but in this matter I am for no half-tide business, and advise a daring stroke. Kidd, you will be best out of business, and can carry out your ideas at small expense on a little farm, or something of that sort."

"Well, sir," said Mr. Kidd, with a hesita- ting air, " I sometimes feel as if I had had enough of business ; and I sometimes fear— though really I need hardly feel ashamed— that my nature is irremediably opposed to mere money-grubbing. I confess that, on the whole, the bank has not treated me very kindly of late ; and positively I shall not be sorry to leave it. I can yet be of consider- able service to the world, and, just now, am particularly interested in agriculture. I should like to retire to a decent place," he continued, in his self-satisfied way, " to have a compact

little farm with medium-sized rectangular
fields, approached by good parish roads ; a
mixed soil, not a set of light, dry, hungry
fields that need a shower every week-day,
and a load of manure on Sundays ; nor
among the twenty-acre heavy-land farmers,
who look as if they had been born in a clay
ditch, who only get a new suit after a good
harvest, and can't sleep if a man owes them
a pound after the day of payment. I should
like a good range of cattle sheds, a bulls' cot,
a calves' cot, a roomy root-shed, with pro-
vender lofts above, a pulping house, and a
double-bay barn with stone threshing-floor.
I should also like a house with some comfortable rooms, fitted, in a measure, for such of
my curiosities as I shall and must retain——"

" He says nothing about being fit for
his wife,". said Mrs. Kidd, sorrowfully.
" He doesn't think so much about me as
about the Persian Jad vase, or the cup of

yellow agate—but I don't want to interfere."

." Confound his curiosities and his wants !"
said the Admiral, with an indignant movement of his feet which caused Ariel to look
up from the carpet where he was stretched.
" A man who spoils a good old business
shouldn't talk so. No doubt you would like
a lofty linen-room, sir ; a laundry and man-
gling-room, warmed with hot-water pipes,
and a brewhouse paved with encaustic tiles?"

" I have lived too long in the world,
Admiral, to expect every comfort I might
wish for," said the banker, good-naturedly ;
"and I know that trouble will not desert me
as a farmer, though I hope it will dog me
less than it has already done. I shall often
have unpleasant weather greeting me when I
draw up my blind ; and perhaps my stack-
yard will show me a paucity of stacks, or
the marks of bad thatching on the few I have,

with gutters down the thatch, and the corn sprouting through."

" And I shall have to work with the eggs and the geese and the cows, I suppose," said Mrs. Kidd with some bitterness, " and go clattering about on clogs !"

" I hope not," said Mr. Kidd, with a slight smile ; " though dairy-maids, like quakers' hats, seem to be getting scarce."

" Well, I am altogether bewildered," said Mrs. Kidd, with another emphatic elevation of her eyebrows.

" Go and take your morning walk," said the Admiral; "perhaps that will set you right."

" Perhaps it will," said his daughter, with a sigh. " I should certainly like to have a few minutes with the doctor ; and I want to see Miss Craggy and Miss Ponditch. I feel almost the same as I do in a bad thunderstorm. Come along, Ariel ; poor dog, I hope the bank won't hurt you !"

" Be cautious among your friends, Bella,"
said the Admiral, as she moved slowly towards the door, followed by the fat dog;
" I'm not sure I have not been a fool to
entrust so much to you. You two have not
asked my advice, as you should have done;
but the time seems to have come when it is
wanted, and will do good. Now, Kidd," he
added, when he was alone with his son-in-
law, " there's no doubt of this—you've made
a sad mess of your business, and your money
matters generally."

" The bank has not been of much pecuniary
benefit to me, on the whole ; but it is rather
a painful subject——"

" Perhaps we can't do much good by talking of it now. Do you agree with me that
this marriage is to be encouraged?"

" It must be a good measure for Storker,
if the proper affection——"

" Yes, yes, et cetera. Now you must try

to gain the help and sympathy of your cousin Oscar. If I am not a fool, the girl would do more at his gentle persuasion than at her mother's bullyings—if M.A. should try that course."

"I think I can manage Oscar," said Mr. Kidd. "You mustn't think that because everything may not be quite satisfactory at the bank—and I confess I have been under a shadow, as it were, for some time—I am wholly and fully a failure. Oscar admits that, in some practical matters, I entirely excel him ; for, as he said of himself the other day, with all respect to Ovid, his deeds are not equal in weight to his words. As to business, too, though I am no money-grubber, I have some considerable capacity. I can make a bargain——"

"For example, with the old spinning-wheels and dressing-machines you bought up ?"

" I grant that they were an unprofitable investment, Admiral; but you would find it difficult to sell me a badly made cart. I can pick you out a pair of good cylindrical wheels. Now Oscar, who can talk——"

" I should not wish to sell you a cart, mister, without having the cash down. But I don't want to hear any words about your practical skill, or Oscar's chatterings and readings."

" Understand me, I don't intend to condemn his readings. I always wish to be fair, and I acknowledge the utility of books. We should no doubt appreciate the kaleidoscope better if we were familiar with Brewster's treatise on it. And, then, Mr. Rack's book——"

" To the devil with the books !" cried the Admiral. " And as to the practical work you have done, where are the fruits of it ? That's all I've got to say."

"Come, Admiral, I have been of use in my time ; and, even in the matter of money, though I have lost it, I have circulated it, I hope, sometimes in channels where it was well appreciated."

"To the devil with such circulation of good money! It's poorly laid out in purchasing such a smattering of practical knowledge as you can boast of."

"Even a smattering is sometimes useful. A clockmaker must have a smattering of carpentry, or he might not hang his wall-clocks accurately. I don't expect ever to regret my knowledge of all the points of distinction between a ledge and a panel door, or my partial acquaintance with galvanism, die-sinking, glass-blowing, and so forth. In view of your suggestions as to my new sphere of life, it is gratifying to me to think that at the age of twelve you could not have made me confuse a twig of wych-elm with

one of witch-hazel, and I could then have
told you that heavy land could be known by
its oak-trees, carlics, and eight-furrow work,
and light land by its Scotch-firs, poppies, and
rabbit-burrows."

The Admiral rose from his chair, angrily.

" In the only good practical work—money
making," he said, with a frown and in bitter
tones, "you are thoroughly beaten by your
bookish cousin."

" It would seem so," said Mr. Kidd, rather
gloomily. " Yet I think that Oscar is too
bookish, notwithstanding his success in business. I can't help thinking that some of the
many hours he spends in his study might be
more profitably devoted to practical life. I
have heard him say that Shakespeare, Scott,
Byron, and others, owe much of their success
to their practical knowledge of the world;
and that Cantacuzenus, Xenophon, Cæsar,
Guicciardini, and I know not who else,

through taking part in the histories they
wrote——"

"Why, man, your cousin goes more often
into society than yourself !" the Admiral
interposed.

" To be frank, he does."

"Yes," said the Admiral slowly, and
pointing from his own smart velvet coat to
the seedy, tobacco-scented garment of his
son-in-law, "and, to his credit, pays more
respect to what he calls 'the minor decencies
of life.' "

" I never liked ceremony. At the same
time, I am not a hermit. Only the other day
I was noticing that hermits were revived in
the same year that pumps were invented ;
and I thought how infinitely less the former
had benefited the world than the latter."

The Admiral smoothed his white hair
with an impatient hand.

" You are as queer a specimen as your

cousin, Kidd," he said, "and that's saying something, on my honour."

" Quite my opinion, ancient," said Storker, entering the room at this moment, followed by Ariel, who had not been equal to the exertion of following his mistress upstairs to the door of her dressing-room. " Both these Ashbockings have some ideas which, if they could be embodied, would be as grotesque as any bird on a Syrian tile, or any griffin in a Moorish palace of Spain !"

" What brings you here, young mister ?" demanded the Admiral, eyeing his grandson grimly.

" I got a little weary of the office, and have come home for a glass of sherry," said Storker, dropping into an easy-chair. " I'm weary of gazing at a table of stamp-duties, and folio after folio of neat writing. I would give a trifle for a canter down a breezy avenue. Mr. Oscar—who is so monstrously odd, some people would doubt whether he is all right in the upper regions—has set me a dry task with some court-rolls of the Manor of Soggs Watering, but has been seasoning it with some queer, but less dry, talk about all sorts of things, such as the archaic classics, Phallic rites, and the Latin styles of Henry of Huntingdon, Milton, Landor, Kuster, and Ruhnken. But I had one other object in coming home, and that is to unburden my mind, which I resolved to do, being an impatient dog, without delay. It seems that I have arrived at a fitting time, Admiral; for I make a shrewd guess you have been talking to my father about certain things announced to myself yesterday."

Mr. Kidd looked uneasily at his son, drew another deep breath, and laid his hand on Storker's arm gently.

" Cheer up, father," said Storker. " But let me pump out my statement. I have been turning and turning my grandfather's words in my mind, and I plead guilty to a change in my ideas as to females, and—perhaps you will hardly believe me—I must assure you that I have always, somehow, instinctively drawn a line between Clara and the others. And, to speak to the point, as my grandfather is so anxious that I should try to persuade Clara to marry me——"

" And wisely," broke in the Admiral; "as you will acknowledge one day, young mister. My words, though few, are not a fool's."

" I will believe that your words on this subject are as full of wisdom as a pot of ditch-water of animalculæ."

" You won't be able to refute my argument easily."

" Perhaps not, sir ; though you are so honest a reasoner that you sometimes reveal the refutations of your arguments as prominently as their supports.   In this case your position is strengthened by beauty to please the fancy, and pecuniary advantage to gratify the judgment. If all works out well, you shall not live in discomfort under my roof. You shall have Roquefort cheese and bachelor's punch, if you wish, for breakfast, and, during the day, shall recline upon a couch, pick out Eliza Acton's best hints for esculent concoctions, and dictate, them to the kitchen through a liveried myrmidon."

" I'm not fond of this town," said the Admiral ; "but I shall live with you, young mister, and I must have my few little luxuries. I'm not a fly who can flutter fantastically about all day after a morning visit to the sugar-basin. And, as to yourself, if this plan of mine comes to a head, you must become a sober and thoughtful fellow. You must use your brains."

" Of course, else they will be of less service than a calf's, which at least make an agreeable sauce. Father," he added, turning to the banker, "in consenting to make myself agreeable to Clara, I am not a little urged on by the belief that my marriage with her will be a comfort to you. I am pretty certain that I can very easily get to like her. Confound it, after all, a man can't keep his passions longer at rest than the earth its winds. I mean to go in for this matter in earnest."

Mr. Kidd pressed his son's hand, and the Admiral poked him in the waistcoat with a short laugh.

"Well said!" he exclaimed; "I will wager Julia Pittock's Madeira to an empty pig-trough that you bowl Hern over. By the way, we have heard that you have, in very truth, a sort of rival in this fellow," he continued, telling Storker, for the first time, of Rebecca Swindell's discovery.

"But we'll annihilate this article," he said,

at the close of his announcement. " I don't
look on him as an obstacle worth considering."

But Storker's countenance was overshadowed, and he vented his feeling in a
low apprehensive whistle.

" I have tried to believe it impossible," he
then said, in a serious tone, "that Hern could
be guilty of this folly.   Dash it, this is too
bad. . He has grit in him, and a good bit of
address ; but he has aimed too high.   Clara
is an uncommon girl, and altogether too good
for him, and the connection with Boulder
will be ruinous to her, and must break her
heart.   By George, this throws some light
on the old fisherman's tactics this morning,
when he encouraged my favourite aspersions
on womankind ; and Hern stood up for the
sex with an earnestness I can now account
for.   Clara shall never lower herself by such
a marriage.   I am not one to worship the

aristocracy; many of the class are proud
paupers, who wear lace and dine on turnips,
as it were; and many are contemptible cur-
mudgeons—but here's my mother, who won't
approve of such a criticism as this."

"I'm glad to see you here, my dear
Storker," said Mrs. Kidd, smiling on her son.

She was dressed, as usual, in very costly
attire, which she had put on after a little
deliberation. "If things are not so good
as they might be at the bank," she had
reasoned with herself, "I'm not to blame,
and I'm still a Howsegoe. Besides, my out-
door dress is never over-gay; for I know too
well my duty as an example to females in a
lower station, who are only too ready to
cover themselves with ribbon tassel and
fringe; and on Sundays, I am sure, my
colours are sober enough, for it's more
Christian to have them so."

After her return, the conversation was prolonged for a few minutes, and she was informed of Storker's determination. She seemed a little comforted, and, again asserting that she was very bewildered, prepared to take 'her walk, Storker proposing to accompany her as far as his route back to the office would allow.

" I don't know what's going to happen," said Mrs. Kidd, as she moved towards the door, " but I hope it will all end well ; and I hope, father, that you won't find any fault with my dress, as well as with my caution. If there's any fault to find, find it now, please, and not behind its back and mine."

" Bother your dress," said the old sailor, gruffly ; " go along, and don't forget yourself among your gossips."

" Gossips ! who is there to gossip with, now that Lady Stowers is from home, Mrs. Monument is ill, and you yourself are going to call on Mrs. Pittock ? Aristocracy is rather a scarce thing in Heathhammock."

" I should say so," said Storker. "A baro-
net might treat a stranger coolly in this place,
without much risk of finding him a prince.
Well, you don't lose much, mother, for few of
your aristocrats have more brains than a
butter-cooler, or minds broader than their
ancestors' graves."

The mother and son then left the house,
and descended the stone steps.

" You walk with consummate deliberation,"
said Storker, " like a true invalid. You should
have a-bath chair; but I dare say you wouldn't
like strangers to think you had, like Erictho-
nius, some personal defect to hide."

" I'm far from well to-day, my dear Storker," she replied ; "how bright the sun is.
I'm not sure my eyes won't become an anxiety
to me, before long. I think I should use some
blue-tinted spectacles, but they are not very
becoming. Oh, I hope we're not going to be
brought down in the world ; but your father

is a funny man, though harmless, I'm sure
(a little too fond of port wine—not that I interfere with him) ; and as to money, we have
spent, no doubt, where we might have spared."

"And there may have been some little
muddling in your department, eh, mother ?"

"Well, yes ; but oh, my dear Storker, I cannot bear the idea of being brought down and
humbled ; for we have always been treated
so respectfully, even since I gave up being a
Howsegoe ; for your father has always received
very great civility, especially from the lower
classes. And there's my position in the church
and choir ——"

"I'm afraid my father has lost some little
money ; but, you see, my grandfather con-
fronts the difficulty boldly, and has roused
himself out of the phlegmatic composure
which sometimes seems to possess him."

"I never saw him so full of energy, except,
perhaps, when Mr. Oxburrow's girl pushed

the perambulator over his toe, when sore;
and then he groaned and stamped, and used
bad words most terribly. He reminded me
to-day of your great-aunt MacSwiney, who
was such a bustling person, and who was found
dead in her pantry in purple velvet, and in a
pool of treacle. You'll be a fortunate man to
secure Clara, my dear Storker."

" Doubtless, and decidedly, if I am to have
a wife at all."

" She's a good girl. Your father said the
other day, when his head was full of his
chemicals, that if he abstracted any part of
her composition, he should return it to be re-
distilled ; but he's a funny man."

"I think she's as good a girl as I could find,
and I have made up my mind to try to
please her, and if possible to secure her, even
if I have to give up my gun and sports, debar
Molock from worrying rats, which he does
admirably, and face Mrs. Oscar's tendencies

to stern economy, with the mould of age upon them."

"I hope you will be happy, my dear Storker; but I feel rather unhappy."

"Come, mother, you are not one to fan yourself with a hearse-plume; we must face the future bravely: possibly it may be brighter for us all than the past. Sometimes my father has looked as if he would accuse a man of insincerity who said 'well done' many times a day; but let us hope his gloomy thoughts will depart with his business."

"I will go and see the doctor, my dear Storker."

"Be careful with him. You had better let him talk to you for an hour about the dorsal vertebræ, or the vidian nerve, than give you any of his physic. You wouldn't bribe me to stuff myself with doctor's rubbish, if you offered me the continent of Asia. Good-bye for the present, I will attend at luncheon punctually."

Within an hour from that time, in the toy-adorned bazaar of Miss Powditch, where the banker's wife was induced to make a small purchase, at a price framed, one would think, on the Crystal Palace standard, she was informed that on the preceding day Clara Ashbocking had been chased from the kitchen by her mother, armed with a carving knife, and that Rebecca Swindell had during the evening discovered this young lady in the act of eloping with George Hern.

CHAPTER IV.

DURING Storker's first day at the office, but few words were exchanged between him and Hern ; but he had a little conversation about the articled clerk with Mr. Creaks, and Amos Splint, the general tendency of which may perhaps be guessed from Storker's concluding remark :

" I agree with you that this very odd sort of favoritism is objectionable, and I don't wonder at you fellows being hipped about it. Dash it all, Hern's very good-natured, and a useful man, no doubt, ; but it's most un-questionably aggravating to see him always smiled upon. It doesn't follow that he should be treated as necessarily superior in every respect, just because he's the governor's pet, any more than that one of the queen's pigs should be praised by butcher and dealer just because it's a royal pig."

Mr. Oscar's reserve towards Hern was not quite so marked as on the preceding day, and as evening drew near, he asked him to come to the study after tea.

Obeying this summons, he found his employer seated at the table with a somewhat troubled countenance.

"Close the door," he said, gently, "and come and sit here in your old place. We will do no work to-night," he added, pushing from before him two little packets of his shorthand writers' notes, respectively endorsed in the Town-clerk's indistinct leisure-time characters "Extracts from Cicero's Defence of Milo," and "Extracts from Butler on the Government of the Tongue." "I'm very sorry for you."

" Thank you, sir."

" Yes, vexed as I am also, I am very sorry for you ; you know the interest I have taken in you, and you know, I think, that I have really a very strong regard for you ; but let us not talk of that. I am going to place myself before you as a friendly counsellor this evening, and to speak very candidly to you. I want you to give up all thoughts of my daughter, and to release her from the unwise compact made between you."

" That, sir," said George Hern, firmly, " I cannot do."

" Would you not do it if my daughter desired it ?"

" I can only release her at her own desire."

" For her sake, I, as her adviser, desire you to do so."

" Her lips alone can persuade me on this point, sir," said Hern, proudly. " I know too well the sacrifice she will make, but she has counted the cost, and will not shrink from it."

" Ah !" said Mr. Oscar, shaking his head, "you young dreamers think you have chosen your lots definitively; but I fear there are obstacles in your way which cannot be overcome. I am sorry," he added, lowering his voice, "but, passing by my own opinion, I must tell you that Mrs. Ashbocking, my careful, sympathetic partner, of whom I know I have just cause to be proud, and in whose judgment I place great reliance, was very much upset by the discovery of Clara's feelings towards you. I thought, during the night, that she would be very ill, she had such troubled dreams. To-day, too, she has been feverish ; and I am afraid that unless you and Clara will consent to break off an engagement which has really many unpleasant sides, the consequences will be very grave to her mother. Mrs. Ashbocking, between our-

selves, is peculiar. She has very strong
opinions upon this matter, and she never lik es
to have her opinions opposed or thwarted in
any matter. Though a little resisting power
is not a bad symptom in human beings (as, I
have heard, it is not in a horse), she won't
countenance opposition from any one under
her influence. She will not, so to speak, leave
her prerogative, as Lord Derby said our
Sovereign does hers, to responsible advisers.
Like James I. of Scotland, she declines to be
content with nominal rule."

" I was afraid Mrs. Ashbocking would
oppose our plans," said Hern; " but I did
not anticipate that she would be made ill by
them."

" She has a queer look in her eyes to-day,
which, positively, I do not like at all."

" I am very sorry to hear it ; but will you
tell me, sir, were you yourself much hurt by
the discovery made yesterday ?"

" Not so much, though one must be cautious, and respect the world's opinions ; not so much. Boulder, poor fellow, to speak very frankly to you, is not quite the sort of connection one would covet for one's daughter, you know."

" Your daughter, sir, is too noble to shrink from him," said George, rather warmly.

" There is a flavour and scent of genuine womanhood in that," said Mr. Oscar; " but we must not disregard the world and its judgment, Hern."

" You would be ashamed of my birth too, sir," said George, with a hurried, anxious glance, and speaking bitterly.

" Never !" said Mr. Oscar, resolutely, and with a kind look at the young man's comely, honest face ; " let the world say what it will on that point. Mantuan's statue, it is true, was placed next to Virgil's, but the misfortune common to him and you has been too often dealt with as a transgression. I shall never

be ashamed of you, my friend; you are at all
times a gentleman."

" I am grateful to you for your kind
words."

" Still, I renew my request as to Clara. I
shall be very glad indeed to see you get on
in life, for you seem to be, as it were, of my
own formation, and I shall certainly take
pleasure in any good stroke made by you ; and
really," continued Mr. Ashbocking, glancing
warily round the room, " I feel that if certain
difficulties could be removed, I (trying to look,
so to speak, into the theory of a man), would
perhaps as willingly give Clara to you, as to
Storker, despite his natural fitness to succeed
me in my business, and his prospects as the
modern 'cambitor' of the town ; and though he
and Clara, have, he says, in old times, prattled
together about being married, like the brothers
and sisters in the hall of Æolus. He seems
an open friendly fellow, but he will hardly

take the place in my regard which you now
hold. Moreover, Mrs. Ashbocking thinks
him in need of improvement. He is not punctual and industrious enough, I doubt, to suit
her; and she was particularly nettled this
afternoon, when he stepped into the house
with a message from his mother, by his sit-
ting down in her favourite chair, to which she
is very partial, though she has not followed
the example of Somerville, Eliza Cook, and
Holmes in addressing verses to it. However,
there is much more intellect in this young
fellow's face than in his grandfather's, and
it quells the expression of sensuality which
seems to have disfigured many of the Howsegoes."

"May I ask, sir, if you think that Mr.
Storker will try to—to win Miss Ashbocking?"

"That's a question I can hardly answer
with confidence; but to speak plainly, I fancy
that he will, for he referred rather warmly to

the rumour (a very unpleasant circumstance), that is floating through the town about you and my poor Clara, and said that he would rather carry his grandfather an English mile, than see Clara degraded into the chronicler of your small beer. He also breathed inuendos against you on other grounds, some of which, I consider, entitle you on the contrary to credit : such as your sacrifice of cricket and football to duty, and your giving up for your work's sake your post in the Life Brigade, or, to quote Storker's language, ‘ in the Royal Standbacks' among whom, by the way, I understand there has been a slight division, arising out of a political argument. Do not think that I blame rational recreation, and ‘ brown exercise,’ for Socrates, Epaminondas, and Cobbett approved of dancing," continued Mr. Ashbocking, who could not refrain from adding three apt quotations from Burton, Hor-rocks and Balzac ; “ but the relinquishment of amusements in your case seemed consistent with the uncommon earnestness which has always more or less distinguished you. I shall never be ashamed of you, George Hern ; you were not, like Hahn, a prodigy at fourteen, but you have some steady and enduring parts (I can sometimes trace, too, certain delicate shadows of imagination in your face), which parts will prove of substantial service to you wherever you go. You have been a valuable servant to me, a useful example to your fellows, though not without your imperfections, and small absurdities, and I cannot help feeling grateful to you, even if you have tried my patience a little sometimes."

" It is for me to talk of gratitude to you."

" As your Mecænas? I have tried to help and benefit you. You have learned much in this room ; and when you are, in the future, denied the like facilities for obtaining knowledge, you must devote all your energies to thinking and reasoning thoroughly, like the younger Malebranche, upon the store you have already acquired. Possibly this course may be preferable to running the risk of having your mind become, like that of the French marchioness, 'a sort of indigestible hotch-potch.'"

"You speak, sir, as if I am to leave you?"

"I fear it must be so, Hern. I shall miss you very much, my friend. I have spent many happy hours in this room with you. You and I have travelled in spirit, so to speak, to many strange and far-off lands, while our bodies have been within these walls. We have been, as it were, as isolated from our neighbours as the Mantchoos. I hardly know what I shall do without you; perhaps I shall leave a multitude of ill-assorted notes, like William Oldys."

"I have been very happy here, sir, too."

"Yes, but our meetings here seem about to be annihilated by a certain other meeting still

more palatable to you, the meeting with my
daughter in the grove summer-house (a fitting place indeed, which Denham might have
praised for its romantic look). But I will not
talk to you about love. I have been more
devoted to matters of the mind than to those
of the heart. At the same time, I can surmise
that you are very unhappy, as is poor Clara,
too : for she is indeed attached to you, and has
told me to-day of your influence upon her."

" And what shall I say of hers upon me ?"

" I can believe it has been great. Speaking
of this room and our work here, I must tell
you that she sometimes coveted your position
as my assistant, but would not for the world
have usurped it, as she thought it was of benefit to you. But, Hern, you must try and root
out your affection, though it pains me to say
so."

" It is ineradicable ; I dare hardly face life
robbed of the old triumphant visions of the

future, which have coloured all my thoughts by day and night."

" Ah, young man, you have yet much wisdom to learn, and my daughter is not yet very wise, I fear. You talk alike."

" I am content to be guided by her wisdom."

"Of course, like a true lover, as Pascal says, you venerate your mistress. I can easily imagine that there is a deep earnestness in this affection of yours which makes it very different from, and superior to, that of some young persons. But, Hern," continued Mr. Oscar, speaking rather hurriedly, " I must not wander from the point. I must counsel you, in the strongest terms, to look your position fairly, and if you can, coldly, in the face. You see a marriage between you and Clara will be disastrous to many. Mrs. Ashbocking, as I have hinted, is horrified at the idea. Clara will be subjected to many and

great inconveniences, and I, who have more
than once been spoken to unpleasantly in regard to my friendship for you, even to the
particular of my letting you pass through the
garden to your lodgings without so much toll-
travers as the asking of leave, shall have to
bear bitter reproaches for having brought this
misfortune upon the family. I say nothing
about the blow it may prove to my reputation and my social position among the
modern East Angles and Iceni, or about the
disappointment to myself as a father—as the
father of such a daughter, I will add—in not
securing her a husband with at least a fair
fortune. I hope I am not mercenary; but
though I have had high dreams and un-
worldly aspirations in my youth, I have
learned to look out for my interest and my
pocket, and am no scorner of 'saint-seducing
gold;' for with all respect to many philo-
sophers, it is very pleasant and very useful,

and brings a man independence and much comfort. You know that I was much gratified last week at having my new will settled by Mr. Bagget Uttridge, my chamber counsel, free of charge, in consideration of the many fees I have placed in his hands. But, to resume, as to my own objections to this marriage, I think it possible that I (who would fain seek out the essential truth and right of things) might be induced to reconsider them. But the feelings and opinions of Mrs. Ashbocking, with whom I have seldom disagreed on any subject but yourself, must be respected. For her sake, and for Clara's, I appeal to you, and indeed for your own."

" Why for my own sake, sir ?"

" Because you are on dangerous ground. Remember what we have read in Quintilian and elsewhere about indiscreet ambition. Because, with better prospects in life than you might have expected, you are drifting into a love affair which, if it fail, will spoil these, and, as it were, turn Heaven and earth into a dreary wilderness. It is true that misfortune sometimes operates as a spur to honest energies ; but not, I fear, such a misfortune as you seem to be preparing for yourself. Johnson says he would never have learned Latin if he had not been whipped (though he also affirmed on another occasion that what we read as a task does us little good). Use your disappointment in its present modified form, like Johnson's whipping, and don't proceed on your perilous course till the crisis, when it comes, falls like a tilt-hammer blow, from which you will hardly recover."

" The postponement of the disappointment will hardly make it greater."

" It may do so. Try at once to let my daughter fade from your mind."

" Impossible !"

" No, no ; you will have an opportunity. She is going to stay with friends away from Heathammock at once. Try to forget her. Make the duty to which you have been so faithful——"

" Owing, God only knows how much, to the good and purifying influence of my feelings towards Miss Ashbocking, and my father."

" I can believe it. But let me now urge you to make that duty, as it were, a lover to you. A dull and unattractive one, you may say ; but I answer that our profession offers not a few attractions to a faithful suitor, if he will not confine himself to its petty details, but will look into its broad principles, and the land-marks of its history. Many lawyers, I doubt not, are ignorant as to the language in which the Treaty of Utrecht and the Year Books of Edward I. are respectively written.

A lawyer should look into the Levitical law,
the Jus Gentium, the Canon law, and the
Civil law ; should especially know something
of the old Roman Juris Consults. In my
copy of ' Blackstone,' you know, there are
quotations from Froben and Thibaut, and
Pushta, and Ortolan, and illustrations drawn
from such widely varying sources as the histories of the kings of Assyria and Turkestan,
Shakespeare and Taylor the water-poet,
St. Louis, Quayle, and Holinshed. But if I
could have my time over again, I would study
upon a wider basis. Possibly some of the
knowledge so acquired might be of small use
in practice, though it might be advantageous
to know enough of agriculture to be spared
the necessity of imitating Confucius in
avoiding one (say a client) who asks counsel
on the subject ; and you might be able to
give satisfaction to a medical client by
quoting Hippocrates concisely (for business

time is valuable), or to a chemical client by quoting Klaproth Dollfuss or Bergman. A dish of legal advice might be made a little more palatable (though I confess I seldom adopt the expedient) by the seasoning of a word or two of useful information on another subject, even though it be a dry one, such as 'the parabolic curve,' or 'cuneiform decipherment,' or a comparison of pure Greek with Hebraisms. A lawyer will not, I think, be in any degree less trusted or appreciated by his clients, if he is able to tell them, in addition to the advice in hand, that the flesh of the gazelle is savoury, or that the Turks wrested Égypt from the Circassians in such a year, or that sand of quartz is congenial to cinnamon shrubs, or that Poe says that perversity is a primitive impulse of the heart, or that grass-wrack produces soda, or that whistling arrows were at one time used to give warning of night attacks, or that Vossius wrote on the Pelasgian controversy, and Vida on chess, and silk-worms, or that the moon is in part unilluminated."

George Hern rose gloomily from his seat, with little inclination to be any longer a spectator of this hobby-riding of his patron.

" I hope, sir," he said, " that after a time, perhaps a long time, of patient effort and good conduct on my part, you may come to think better of my pretensions."

But Mr. Oscar Ashbocking only shook his head ; and they parted.

CHAPTER V.

VERY shortly after Hern's departure, though not before Mr. Oscar Ashbocking had pencilled one more passage in his copy of Herm Hugo's " Pia Desideria " (which he had already annotated almost as richly as Boyle did his " Spenser "), the front-door bell was rung vigorously. He could not hear the timid step of Trippington on her way to answer it, but caught the deep voice of Boulder. He expected to detect some interference on the part of his wife, but before this could take place, the great fisherman stood in the study doorway.

" Sarvent, sir," he said.

"I am not sure I can candidly say I am glad to see you, Boulder," said the town clerk, suavely, "for I have already spent a good deal of this evening in talk. Do you come with the intention of staying some time ? If so, please to close the door."

Boulder obeyed, thus demolishing his companion's hopes of his early departure.

"I know, sir," he said, "that my poor boy come from this here house just now. I've been troubled in my mind about him, an' I've made so bold as to come an' speak to you. One can't cast lead too much with ugly coast, thick weather, an' lively water."

"Well, sit down, Boulder."

"Thank you, sir ; I wish you well, sir."

The fisherman accompanied these last words with a gesture as of raising a vessel to his lips, and Mr. Ashbocking, taking the hint, produced some mild sherry, a decanter of which he always kept in his study.

" Here's towards you, sir," said Boulder,
quickly despatching his glassful; "I'm a
temp'rate man, but I'm a little down to-night,
an' I ain't one to drink a sight at my own expense, for I'm careful o' my moneys, an', as
you know, a layer-by."

" Most creditably so."

" An' my trade, sir, ain't the best o' trades
to lay-by a sight out of. A fisherman's, sir, is
often a devilish dirty look-out."

" In other words," said Mr. Ashbocking,
" you endorse the statement of Moschus : ' Ill
fares the fisher on his ocean way,' and agree
with Sappho when she called the life of Pel-
argon, who, as you do, claimed St. Nicholas
as his patron saint, ' A hard and poor one.' "

" No doubt but what you're right, sir,"
said Boulder, " I allays run down the sea
afore my boy ; but, between ourselves, I ain't
sure I've any great call to grumble, considerin'
there was a time, not so very long ago, when

I couldn't lay a fi' pun' note on a flap-table,
an' say 'that's mine,' and now I've got four
good boats, an' the biggest, the *George Hern,*
is the best beach-boat hereabouts."

"I am glad you feel satisfied with your
occupation. Seafaring is a very necessary
branch of what Collins calls, 'Far-fatiguing
trade;' for, to quote Centlivre, 'The merchant
is for traffic everywhere.'"

"Ay, ay, sir ; but, as you know, it 'ont do
to talk o' the sea, an' that like, afore George.
Breath o' my body ! it's made me turn cold
sometimes to hear him talk o' the *Mayflower*
an' the *Endeavour,* an' the *Erebus* an' the
Terror. He's got a sperrit which he in-
herited from me, though, as he say, I wouldn't
ha' willed it to him, if it had bin a matter o'
willin'. But the sea's bin an ole friend to
me, an' not a bad 'un. I've wrought hard,
for there's no play about me, and I've bin
careful o' my moneys ; an' I think I've done

my duty by my son. But now, sir, there's a great fresh trouble ahid, an' he seemed to think this morning that I'd best not interfere, tho' it's the fust trouble of his as I've bin kep' from, an' I don't feel to wish to keep out o' this. Old heads are better 'an young 'uns in many things, but he's grown a little uppish, is George."

"Young people seem to recognise few things sooner than their own approach to manhood. Philip Augustus wanted to rule at the age of fifteen, for instance."

"I didn't think so much o' myself when I'd a four-inch beard as this lad do now. He mustn't think he can do everything without his old father, sir," Boulder added warmly.

"Don't excite yourself, Boulder. I know you can't brook contradiction, and I know your affection for your son is very strong, but don't be severe with him ; remember he is not a child, and that the subject (I can guess to what you allude) is a delicate one. You must act cautiously and with tact. The mighty Jove changed himself into a cuckoo to gain his point once."

" He mustn't try to do without me, sir, for I've done a sight for him. He mustn't forget that."

" I can guess that you don't quite agree with Cato, that your good actions should go unrewarded. Let me assure you of my firm belief that your son will never prove ungrateful to you, and never do you any great discredit."

" Well, sir, thank you for that—thank you for that," said Boulder, striking the table with his heavy hand ; " I know it well."

" I always acknowledged that he was different to the majority of youths."

" Different !" cried Boulder. " As different as a frigate's hawser from a bootlace or a bit o' g'loon. An', once more, I thank you, sir, for givin' him such a scholard's larnin', an' for all your kindness."

" I wish I could induce a few others to improve their scholarship."

" I wish my boy to get larnin'," said Boulder, shaking his head, " but, if all do that, an' all get the upper hand, who's to clean decks ?"

" Your decks would be cleaned none the less efficiently, I hope, for the spread of knowledge among your underlings. I can't think that a knowledge, for instance, of the origin of the word 'forecastle,' or of Tacitus' definition of a yarn being ' *compositum miraculi causâ*,' or of the mighty influence of Constantinople on the history of shipping, would impair the usefulness of your friends among the fisher-folk or in the mercantile marine ; or that some acquaintance with hydrostatics, or the writings of such men as Peltier, or some familiarity with Noah's primitive vessel, St.

Paul's voyages, the ancient basket-shaped ships of the Saracens, or the marvellous craft of the middle ages, would make a man less valuable as a practical sailor of to-day."

"I don't know nothin' about these things, sir," said Boulder, rather impatiently. "The man who'd know these sort o' things 'ud be a rum 'un, if he weren't a goose-head into the bargain ; an' so much larnin', I should think, 'ud drive such things as scuppers an' bunkers out of a man's noddle. But now, sir, after all this cruisin' round the point, am I to have to thank you for helpin' this boy out of this here new trouble that's rumourin' about in the matter of your daughter ? Are you goin' to be on his side ?"

"I have been dreading your allusion to this subject, my friend," said Mr. Oscar uneasily. "To put you in possession of the fact at once, I will tell you that I can hold out no hope to you of this ill-starred engagement being perfected by marriage. I cannot consent to such a match, and Mrs. Ashbocking, to whose opinions I always pay great deference, is still more strongly opposed to it. I am very sorry for your son."

Boulder uttered an oath, and shifted his chair back vehemently.

" I am indeed very sorry," continued Mr. Oscar; "I would rather pay—or, let me say, I would rather do almost anything—learn, for instance, a thousand verses of the 'moral Gower,' than see this youth borne down with a great trouble."

" And so would I," said Boulder grimly; "only I'll do more 'an you, for I'm afeard it's all up, for the lad's set so firm on the lady (not that I wished it), an' it 'ill be a great trouble, and a cruel 'un. He's a man, every inch of him, an' 'ud hold up his arm to be broke, if need be, an' then look at it, calm as a lapwing at the tossin' waves ; but I've lost

my mark if this thing 'ont knock him out o'
time."

"No, no. As Seneca says, 'a wreck does
not stop a seaman from putting to sea again.'"

"God forbid my boy should put to sea
at all."

"You misunderstand my allusion. He will
overcome this disappointment, though great—
for he is not a man to form lukewarm attach-
ments, I think."

"I know it well; look what he's bin to
me."

"All must admire the good feeling that has
existed between you. I have often been
glad for both your sakes. It was good for
George to have an object to warmly interest
his heart while his brain was exercised so
much. Besides, as he acknowledges, his
affection has been an urgent prompter to
industry, and has inspired in him a whole-
some inveteracy of purpose."

" Till this mornin', he's all'ays bin more or less so good to me that I've sometimes thought I didn't deserve it all, for I've disgraced him more 'an once."

"Love and warm goodwill could supply the place of lessened respect. Your chief offences, too (setting aside 'drunkenness,' or as the Romans wisely call it, 'absence,'), would hardly be without a tint of heroism in the view of the young."

" There's a blood-an'-thunder sound about 'em, eh?" said Boulder, gloomily. " But they're bad to look back on for me—passion, an' blasphemy, an' violence, an' such like."

" A Chinese witness gives emphasis to his oaths by the peaceful breakage of crockery ; but I have heard that you have been seen wrathfully breaking furniture, and swearing terrific oaths at the same time. However, we won't talk of these things."

" No, sir, no ; I go to church for sarmuns, an' aint very fond of 'em there, aither."

" Perhaps because they sometimes reproach you. Æschines called some of the eloquent words of Demosthenes 'impudence and mar-vellous knavery,' because——"

" I don't want so many sarmuns to set me square," said Boulder, impatiently ; " nor yet no beadle to lead me, specially if he be like our beadle Skinner, who have smoked so much, his inside must be like a chimbly ; an' for that matter, I don't want no parson Audrey, nor yet no curate Kidd.'

" As to Mr. Kidd's sermons," said Mr. Ashbocking, " I grant they are somewhat dull ; they would never gain him such a happy name as his poems did Firdousee ; nor have they even the charm of quaintness, which, in a measure, reconciles us to such discourses as those of Richard Taverner."

" You're too larned for me, sir," said Boulder, in a tone of mild despondency; " I can't take it in like the boy George."

" Well, Boulder, to quote Ben Jonson, I desire not to outrun the apprehensions of my auditory."

" All I can say is," said Boulder, "I must be thankful I've managed to keep myself pretty well in check o' late years. Now an' agen I've bin hard tempted, but I've stood ; an' the boy know all, for we've kep' nothin' from each other, an' so it ain't pleasant, don't you see, to think he's goin' to hide this love matter of his—capsided though it's like to be."

" He would only conceal as much as pru-dence enjoined, Boulder. There's very little slyness and deceit about him. You will seldom hear from him revelations of hidden follies and errors to lessen and sour affection."

" Ay, ay; but we keep beatin' about the bush. I come here——"

At this moment the door opened, and the

town-clerk, not a little to his relief, saw his wife enter. She was stern in look, and, as usual, plain in dress. She did not offer Boulder any greeting, but, turning to her husband, said, in a tone which was the involuntary exponent of half-suppressed excitement :

" You are having a good deal of conversation this evening. It is getting late."

" Yes, Mary Ann," said Mr. Oscar, mildly. " Boulder, as you might guess, has been talking about his son."

" The less said about him the better, I should think," she retorted, glancing searchingly at Boulder, and then at the empty wine-glass near him.

" I never was, an' never will be ashamed to talk about him, be it to you or be it to any other male or female," said Boulder, warmly.

" This is hardly the time to bring his

name forward in this house," she answered, bitterly, and beginning to arrange in hasty fashion the books within her reach; " he has cast a shadow here which neither he nor you will ever be able to appreciate or understand. Mr. Ashbocking will allow me to tell you (for your son has not taken away all my influence), that he does not like to have his readings interrupted, or to have visitors in this room."

" He has my own son here often enough," said Boulder, sulkily.

" There is a distinction between you and your son," said Mrs. Oscar; " and more than I like," she added to herself.

" It's true I ain't larned," said Boulder.

" Nor are you over civil; not that I am a person to be awed by roughness. I have a strong mind."

" I know I ain't gentleman enough for you; but I'm clean."

"Considering your occupation, I grant you are."

" That is at least satisfactory to Mrs. Ashbocking," interrupted the town-clerk, with a smile ; "she would almost excuse Mohammed for roasting Christians on account of his love of cleanliness ; though, by-the-way, she once grudged me a morning bath, when I mistook a bit of Swiss muslin for a towel (not that my ' objective regards ' often play me false)."

" I'm for cleanliness, anyhow," said Boulder. "Any one who had much to do with George mustn't be content with a lick an' a promise, as they say. So, ma'am, we are o' one opinion there."

" I have given no opinion," said Mrs. Oscar, curtly.

" No, I dessay you think opinions are things to be bought at a lawyer's for a fee."

" If Mr. Ashbocking wastes good time in

giving you gratuitous opinions at this part of
the day, I say he is doing rather a foolish
thing."

" Suppose he is," said Boulder.

" No, I don't allow you to suppose so,"
said Mrs. Ashbocking, excitedly. " You
come and trouble him out of office hours, and
I don't wonder that he does not exercise all his
usual tact. But I won't hear a word against
him from you ; if you think I will, you do a
foolish thing."

" And don't you ever do a foolish thing,
ma'am ?"

" Perhaps so. I did one very foolish thing
when I agreed that Mr. Ashbocking should
treat your son with such uncommon friendli-
ness and indulgence."

" He was worth it all," said Boulder,
angrily ; "he's wrought well for you together,
an' for himself too. Hard rubbin', I know,
don't all'ays mean polishin' ; but his hard

work have made him a man to be proud of. He was worth all you done for him."

"You needn't think that I do not know enough of fathers and mothers to guess that you would make such a reply. Why don't you tell us that your son is a genius ? It's lucky for you that he is nothing of the kind ; for your small genius, I believe, is generally a fool who runs into debt, and foists his children for support on his more sober friends. The only genius I ever knew was William Doggles, who, after being a bankrupt grocer, became an organist and photographer, with one meal of meat a week."

"A man of genius," said Mr. Oscar, "who, like 'walking Stewart,' according to De Quincey, is not also a man of talent, is apt to be misunderstood and ill appreciated."

"Your son is a decent youth," continued Mrs. Oscar, more calmly, to Boulder; "but

considering his parentage and so on, I beg
to say, whatever Mr. Ashbocking may have
remarked to you, that it will be better for
him to leave this place before more trouble is
brought about.   I was never quite of the
same opinion as Mr. Ashbocking concerning
him, and it would have been well if my views
had prevailed.   As it is, the boy has now
aimed at a mark out of his reach.   He might
have been contented, I should have thought,
with being petted in a manner few in his
situation could expect, without aspiring to a
girl who has not her equal in this part of the
world, and causing her name to be mixed up
with his in every gossip's mouth.   I have
given my silly meddling servant a sound
scolding for hinting to Swindell of what took
place between me and my daughter yesterday.   You might as well give news to the
town-crier for publication as to him, when his
daughter is at home.   There, I don't wish

to talk incautiously, but I have spoken my mind. I wish to make no enemies, but I am genuine; and it is useless to try to be agreeable to all people. If you lay yourself out to suit A, and then to suit B as well, they may find some disagreeable inconsistencies if they ever compare notes. Oscar, I should despatch this friend at once."

With that she stepped hastily from the room, Boulder glaring at her figure as she retreated, and afterwards at the door.

" Curse the woman !" he exclaimed. " If she warnt your missus, sir, I'd call her something. I'll——"

" Don't rail and threaten, Boulder," said Mr. Oscar, kindly. " Reason is a better weapon than the edge of the sword. I must not allow any uncomplimentary allusion to Mrs. Ashbocking. She has spoken in all sincerity ; for if she has a little of the cynicism of Demetrius, she has much of his invulnerable honesty. But, like Simo in 'The Fair Adrian,' she doesn't always regard civility in carrying out her purposes."

Boulder paused a few moments, and wiped his face, which was somewhat flushed by his excitement. Then he vociferated—

" I say that the boy's worthy o' what's bin done for him, and worthy o' your daughter. Maybe I'm over-proud of him, but I say he's worthy ; an' I on'y ask his due—not so much as a ole door-mat or a little straw above the mark. I on'y ask two fardens for my ha'penny, an' not the vally o' my thumb-nail over."

" We will talk no more of this to-night. Go home now."

" Can't you give me any hope to carry home, afore I trip my anchor ?"

" I dare not give you any hope. I wish I could. I have admired your resolute reformation of character, my friend, and I would willingly give you some practical proof of my esteem and friendship. Moreover, I have never forgotten how well you protected my father in the small church-rate riot here, years ago."

" As to fightin', I could lend a hand well enough ; but that ain't, as you may say, the title-deed to much good i' this world. Most folks want handlin' more like a bird's egg than a ship's cable. A mere fighter's no use. So you can't give me any hope, sir ?" he continued, stopping an allusion to Catiline which hung on the tongue of his companion.

" No. But I hope to remain your friend, and your son's friend, for many years."

Boulder sat silent for a short time, and then rose.

" I think you wish me well, sir," he said, more calmly. " There be some folks that are great folks ; but to mix up with 'em don't dignify a man, no more 'an it dignify a hog to be potterin' about among the cows. But it's somethin' to be hand an' glove with you, if one can tackle the larnin'. But my boy 'ud never disgrace you, sir, for he's every inch the gentleman, an' as fit for your daughter, sir, as that there fat son o' Mr. Kidd, an' more too. It ain't that I trouble so much myself, sir, about this here marriage business—for I've made the boy a gentleman, an' don't look no further—an' I hope this love affair 'ont spoil my work, but that he'll come round to his senses an' his duties after a bit; for though the ripple seem to be creepin' into the boat, there's hope still; an' instids o' cursin' a foggy mornin' we should remember it's good for sprattin'."

"Well said, Boulder. And now, good-night. But first, let me fill your glass again. You can return to your lodgings through the garden."

Of this permission the fisherman availed

himself, as Mr. Swindell never fastened his two garden-barriers, there being no lock or bolt upon either of them.

The sky was overcast and starless; and as Boulder passed along the path which lay parallel with the front of the house, and which reached almost to the high side-wall before it joined the narrower gravel walk down the garden, his eye was attracted by a light flickering, in broken gleams, through some matted and thickly-leaved branches, close to the ground, at the extreme end of the house. It came from the window of the last of the underground rooms, and this window was separated from the pathway by a corner-bed, on which stood a partly withered larch tree, supposed to be nearly a century old, and a dusky company of shrubs.

" What's that ?" muttered Boulder. " If it's old Swidger among the grub, she might as well give me a slice o' somethin' to put

with the governor's sherry. But I doubt if
she durst, wi' such a cat of a missus."

He made his way, with some difficulty,
towards the window, and peered through its
dirty panes. Within was evidently a lumber-
room, with a grim and musty medley of contents, among which the fisherman's sharp eye
could detect ancient clothes, gloves, bottles,
corks, and pieces of string ; the headless and
mutilated trunk of a stuffed puff-adder, the
remains of a galvanic battery, a peacock's
feather, a cup of dried-up paste, a little figure
of lead, a brown scratch-wig, a cat-skin cap,
a boot with a wooden sole, a portion of a
stout spruce ladder, a tin candlestick, and
some candle-ends, so discoloured that neither
rat nor Esquimaux could have been tempted
to set teeth in them. On the brick window-
sill, beside the burning candle, lay an old
bonnet, holding, it seemed, oak-apples,
acorns, beech-nuts, keys, shells, match-boxes,

disused quill pens, and fragments of sealing-wax.

But the watcher's attention was soon arrested by a human figure, that of the lady of the house, who, stretching her right arm up the chimney, brought down, in her gloved hand, not without a strong effort, a stained linen bag.

Placing this on the floor, and untying its mouth, she took from it a handful of sovereigns, upon which she gazed, till her stern lips broke into a smile, and her eyes glittered with satisfaction.

Then she replaced the coins, took from her pocket a sovereign to add to the store, set her teeth firmly, and, summoning all her strength, lifted the bag to its hiding-place again.

The exertion was so great that she sat down upon a ragged cowhide box to rest; and, meanwhile, amused herself by peeping at a file of old receipted bills, occasionally repeating an item aloud, such as, "Sack of household—two pounds thirteen," "Half of log-wood—fivepence farthing." Very soon, however, she had risen and left the lumber-room, locking the door behind her, we may be sure.

So Boulder discovered that, well as this lady understood and appreciated the fruits of wise investments, it pleased her to have a little store with which neither banker nor borrower could interfere.

CHAPTER VI.

THE face which George Hern turned from his book when his father entered their sitting-room at Sunrise Lodge was a pale, earnest, and weary one, but his voice was strangely calm and deliberate.

" I think I can guess where you have been, father," he said.

" Well, it ain't often I'm out o' nights after I come home from the beach," said Boulder, " unless I'm after some inland business."

" You have been occupying yourself with business of mine. You have been to Mr. Ashbocking's ?"

" Yes, an' the rights of it, too—why not ?"

said Boulder sharply. " Who's to blame me ? But I'd no luck, and Mrs. Swab Ashbockin' tried to sit on me."

" I have been picturing these things to myself."

" Ay, ay," said Boulder impatiently and satirically ; " o' course you have—you're a clever chap, an' afore me by long chalks in much. But there's no man's afore another in everything."

" I agree," said George quietly.

" What ails the boy ?" cried Boulder, looking hard at him. " This mornin' obstrep'rous, an' now as flat as Flanders. I ain't goin' to sit on you, George, nor yet to put my know agen yours. God forbid you should want to learn the teachin' that come to you in a fearful nor'-westerly gale in the Bay o' Biscay, or in such a one as I had to face once sailin' from Jamaiky, latitude 38 north, longitude 60 west. What ail you, lad ?"

" I told you this morning, father, that in—
in this one matter I wished you not to take any
part just yet," said George, closing his book
and rising. " But I have been giving myself
a strong dose of thought and reasoning and
self-examination this evening, and I have
come to doubt whether there can be a sound
core in any movement I may make which I
could wish to keep hidden from you, which
shall make the first breach, however small,
between two such good friends as we have
been. I am speaking very earnestly, though
in few words, father, when I say that most
heart-rending, most bitterly disappointing, as
seems the sacrifice I am trying to face, most
deeply as I love Miss Ashbocking, and most
joyfully as I would welcome her as my wife,
I must turn from this bright picture rather
than from you !"

Boulder seized his hand.

" By God, you're a man an' a hero : but,

p'r'aps, you needn't turn from ayther, lad,"
he said.

George sat down again and rested his forehead upon his hands.

" There are shadows in the picture, father,
I fear," he said after a short pause, " but I
won't turn to them now. Let us say no
more to-night. Be assured of this, father,"
he continued, rising, with a firm look, though
his smile was faint, and shaking the fisherman's great hand, " I will hold to you faithfully and fast, as you have held to me.
Good-night."

Before Boulder, pleased by his son's words,
yet half-puzzled by his extreme seriousness
of demeanour, could make any further rejoinder, the young man had left the room.

Before the latter rose on the following day,
Boulder, by appointment, started for Southaston, where he remained all day. When he
came home in the evening he found that

George, complaining of headache, had taken a walk, leaving a message for him that he should choose the Raddiston road. He guessed that his father would set out to meet him, if he returned home during his absence, for a walk admitted of conversation, which the young lawyer's studies usually curtailed at home. His surmise was right, for Boulder hurriedly despatched some bread and butter and a mug of tea, and then marched down the town.

He had reached the Lug-sail Inn, but was here brought to a stand, for from the tap-room window came the sound of his own name.

" Between ourselves, and speakin' private-like, I ain't goin' to say but what he's done well by the young chap, for all it's made him as mean as the devil, an' has made both father and son precious uppish, an' different to other folk," said the voice of Mr. Bayard

Swindell, in tones which justified the popular saying that a Heathhammock undertone was something like a shout; "but this here up-start sort o' love affair 'ud damn the boy an' undo all the ole man's doin'ses, if it warn't altogether too much o' the monkey, as you may say, to be thought on serious."

"The ole man's doin'ses are somethin' wonderful," said another voice; "an' specially considerin' he's a fisherman, which, as the publicans 'ill bear me out, are the most spendin' chaps in the world."

"Boulder's doin'ses ain't so bad," continued Mr. Swindell; "but I'll lay any one o' you here a suvren to a shillin' he don't pay all the money down, which he've set himself to do, at the end o' the five year, nor yet within six month after that!"

"I 'ont take you, that's sartin," said Mr. Mumbles, the landlord. "It's like this here: I think I can lay out my shillin' better; an' as to Boulder, it's little good he do me or the trade."

The listener could not hear the next remark ; for a hand was laid on his shoulder, and he saw Mr. Bilge standing by his side.

"What, are you tempted just to go in for once ?" said the sleek butler, with his ready smile. " Come, sir ; I was goin' in myself for a few minutes I've got to spare. There was a time when you was one o' the best o' the company in there, you know. Come in, sir."

" I will," said Boulder, sternly ; " for there be folk in there as I may hev to speak to."

The Lug-sail was the most popular resort in Heathhammock. It was a " free " house, and the liquors sold were good, whereas all the other small inns were " tied " houses, belonging to Mr. Oxburrow, of the Earl of Sandwich Brewery ; and an opinion prevailed that his malt drinks were some-

times only second-rate when they issued
from his premises, and that his prices made
an occasional dilution on the part of the
profit-seeking publican expedient. Moreover, the owner of the "Lug-sail," Mr.
Mumbles, a retired pedlar, was a man of
tact, who had even ingratiated himself somewhat into the favour of females, those drag-
weights on the publican's prosperity. The
well-known complimentary address he used
to bellow to the fair sex, when he was a
pedlar, still lingered in the memories of many
house-wives, "Here's your ready-money
man, for the bright-eyed angels of the household!"

In the little taproom here, every evening,
amid a strong scent of tobacco smoke and
hot and cold potations, much in the condition and prospects of Heathhammock
was discussed and questioned, with an
interest which a far larger portion of the

two hemispheres might be contented to command. But the gossip was tainted with a strong alloy of falsehood and scandal ; and Lord Chesterfield's rule, that we should not speak of ourselves, was by no means regarded at the Lug-sail Inn.

The taproom was almost full when Bilge and Boulder entered it, the company including one of Mr. Oxburrow's draymen, whose rubicund countenance and apron of hop-sacking you would rather have expected to see in one of his master's houses.

Silence at once followed the appearance of the fisherman, and he sat down near the door.

" Bring me a pint o' gin-an'-beer, mate," he said, looking gloomily at Mr. Mumbles.

" Let me stand that drink, Mr. Boulder," said Bilge, suavely, " seein' that I brought you in."

" You may stand, sure enough," said

Boulder. "I'm careful o' my moneys. But
I should ha' thought some of these here
good folks could better stand, as they, some
of 'em, seem to have so much money to risk
in bets about me," he added, looking round
with a glance no one seemed willing to meet.
" I heerd you, Mr. Swindell."

The gardener appeared to be a little con-
fused ; but, after a short pause, and with a
sulky stare at the floor, he said—

"Whatever you heerd, I don't mean any
disrespect, an' I on'y give an opinion."

" No, that's all, Mr. Boulder," said the
landlord ; "an' opinions are opinions, an'
free, current coin to pass about, you know.
I never knew but what a Briton might give
his opinion free, sir."

" Nor yet I," said Mr. Swindell, doggedly.
" Don't you tell me that, Mr. Boulder. You
may tell that to the chaw-bacons, but not to
us here in Heathhammock."

"No doubt but what you're larned folk here," said Boulder, "an' know coal from clinker. But as to Heathhammock, though you're dorgrapper, and what not, I say it's a 'nition poor parish. An' I say that the · grocer up street, with a matter o' twelve cheeses in his cellar, he's what I call a sort o' type an' figgor o' this parish. An' it's my belief there never was a fifty-pun' note in the place that was not the Ashbockins'; or if there was, Mrs. Scrab Ashbockin collar'd it, or it was blowed into the ocean. It aint for such as live in this parish to be bettin' about whether a man which got his money out o' the great sea can pay his dues or not."

"There's some here besides you which gets their livin' out o' the sea," said Mumbles, pointing out Pilot Buzzard, a couple of fishermen, and Aaron Varnal, a coast-guard, with livid scurvy-scars on his hands, "an' maybe, these have been talkin' about you, too."

"What's the odds o' talkin', mate ?" said Varnall mildly. "I don't want to quarrel with you, an' don't you with me. Let folks talk about me, I say—them as know me know my ways, and them as don't don't sin- nify."

"I 'ont quarrel with you, Aaron," said Boulder, "but curse these chattering fools here. There ain't one o' 'em hev wentur'd so near to death as you an' me. But I 'ont mind their talk any more an' if it was the noise o' pigs or babbies. There was a time when I'd ha' knocked that Swindell through a winder."

"We 'on't talk o' knocks and blows here," said Varnall. "We sea-folks are like to be rather rough dogs, but the land-lubbers, who don't know no more 'an ole crabs about the Naval Discipline Act, nor yet about the ole

Articles o' the Navy, must excuse a bit o'
that. We see a deal o' rough work, an' that
tell its tale. I was aboard the *Neptun'* line-
o'-battle ship, that was tugged out o' Spit-
head in March, '54——"

" That's very well known to us," said Mr.
Swindell sulkily.

" Well, I 'ont bother you with yarns," said
the cheerful coast-guard, " so we 'ont quarrel
on that score, nor yet on any other. An' as
to Boulder, here's luck to him and to his pays
and to his son—for he's a son to be proud
of; an', if he's a oddish chap in some things,
there's somethin' simple, an' straight, an'
downright about him, an' more generosity
than malice ; an' he's got a jolly smile. He'd
ha' made a good seaman, but he's made a
good landsman, for he an' his master hev
got between 'em the best larnin' o' these
parts."

" Thank you, Aaron," said Boulder; " but

I don't care to hear my son talked about at all in this here place."

"And why not," said Mr. Mumbles, rather hurt. "He's only a human being, when you've said an' done all, and we're all human beings here."

"That's poor arguin'," said Boulder in a tone of disgust. "You might as well tell me that a butcher's slop is made o' starlin's eggs because they are both blue."

"Let's change the subject," said Mr. Bilge in a smooth voice. "Our Mr. Storker said he should come to see you soon, Mr. Mumbles, an' taste the Circean cup, or some such cup. He's a queer fish, an' eat an' drink as hearty as the ole Admiral."

"I'll be glad to see him," said the landlord, "an' it's like this here, he can't do better, for he 'ont get here such a glass o' beer as I got this mornin' at a house not far off, which had a twang o' foisty cask, and for strength might ha' been the ninth wort from a peck o' malt."

" I rather think this here Mr. Storker 'ill put Master Hern's nose out o' joint," said Swindell grimly; "though that young wonder look out for hisself pretty sharp. I ain't afraid to speak out, Mr. Boulder, for it's like enough things hev happened which 'ill make me give you a notice to quit. You must thank your son for it. He think hisself good enough for the best o' places, even if it be Presiden' o' the Petty Bag, or some such orfice."

· " It's a pity to talk o' this young man here," said Mr. Mumbles, " for it's like this here, Mr. Boulder don't understand the humours o' the place."

" I ain't so sure about puttin' noses out o' joint, an' improvements, an' fresh folks, an' that like," said Luke Grindstone, the carrier, who looked upon new residents as likely to be in sympathy with the long-expected railway scheme, which would alter his mode of living, if it did not seriously prejudice his fortunes. "I like the ole ways and the tried ways, an' not to have sons thinkin' theirselves better 'an their fathers, an' that like."

"Our Mr. Storker's father's a very decent man in some respects, though soft in some," said Bilge ; "an' in point o' learnin', which you spoke of, Mr. Varnall, he ain't altogether a duffer. He'll tell you about the equatorial currents, an' the theogerlite which they use for the Ord'nance, an' about the Chinese buildin's o' bamboo, an' the Japanese who make everything from a house to a han'kerchief o' paper. He's a queer man."

"Haven't you got anything new to make us laugh about him, Mr. Bilge ?" asked William Dady, commonly called "Strike Dady," he being a striker in the employ of Mr. Peddlegrave, the ironfounder and engineer.

Bilge looked slyly at Boulder, and the latter understood his glance.

"Another pint o' gin an' beer, landlord," he said in a loud tone; "an' the devil take all the talk about my boy's nose bein' put out o' joint by a chap that's more fit for a crazy monkey's tricks. An' as to Mr. Bilge an' his backbitin', let me tell all you here that what I've heerd you talk about me behind my back make me feel more strong what I've often felt before when I've heerd such folks as this here Bilge runnin' down their betters. I hold with my son on this point." •

"I think it's hard a man mayn't give his opinion on any body, just because he ain't lucky enough to have so much money," said Bilge, "keepin' it private, o' course."

"It ain't manly to be smilin' an' stoopin' down to tie a man's shoe-strings one minute, an' to be loadin' him with contempt behind his back the next," said Boulder. " Besides, it ain't noways right for one who call hisself a Christian, an' sit in church, like you do, in sight of his master as prim as a new yacht, to be so full o' venom in secret. You should ha' bin a Methody," he continued, poking the butler with his great fist, "you an' that there other reformed character, Mr. Swindell. What a dinner you'd take out o' the innicent brother as boarded you o' Sunday on your roun's. You'd lay in a week's supplies, if you didn't sniggle some into your pocket—though you mightn't find a tex' to beare you out in that." •

Bilge looked round at the faces of his companions, and seeing grins of merriment on several of them, began to show traces of the wrath and gall of which his bosom was not destitute, despite his many smiles.

" It's leastways pleasant to some of us," he

said, shrugging his shoulders, "to see you
goin' back, in a manner, to your old way o'
jokin', Mr. Boulder. But you fisher folk aint
perfect, you know. There's Mr. Parkins
was one of you once, an' afterwards worked
under a contractor of the railways, and he
says, says he, 'better twenty navvies to look
to than three fishermen ; for,' says he, 'the
fishermen they're intorrerble.'"

"We're an independent set," said Boulder,
"an' we don't have no need to spake agin
our betters, for no man's our master, or give
us biddin', and more's the job for me when I
want a crew for life-boat practice. On'y, let
me speak the truth, where there's life to save,
which is somethin' more 'an practice, a crew
'll come scurryin' up to the ole boat as quick
as a cat across the street."

"Salvage money's handy, ain't it, sir ?"

"You mustn't put it all to that ; though

may-be we ain't so ready to 'work, like the magistrates, without pay an' stipend."

" If you was," said Mr. Swindell, "it ud be so much the better for my bet if anyone had took it. But I'd like to know what right you've got to say this, that, an' the t'other agin my brother-in-law. His character, I'm thinking, 'ud show better 'an yours before any judge o' the land ; and I ask the opinion o' any man here on that point."

" We 'ont go into a man's past doin'ses," said Aaron Varnall.

" The judges o' the land can't see inside a man's waistcoat," said Boulder, "or they might say somethin' that wasn't all pretty to lots of us ; and they might tell Mr. Bilge that, for all his greasy hair, an' the amiableness of his great tater-trap of a mouth, he worn't a sight better 'an a Turk ; that he worn't no better 'an a dirty collier in his heart, for all his decent outsides I'll be bound you're often thinkin', now-a-days, o' the ins an' outs o' poachin' an' liggerin' for pike in preserved waters, an' trespassin' to set snares i' the owl-holes o' barns. Landlord, six o' rum! I want to drink to this here pair o' model brother-in-laws."

" I 'ont hev your drinks," said Mr. Swindell, warmly ; " an', I'm thinkin', you'd best remember that p'r'aps I haven't changed altogether in the matter o' strength an' fist-work."

" It's time you changed in the matter o' pluck, for you never had no more in you than a pea-pod."

" Ah, Mr. Ready-tongue, you'll soon be makin' a fool o' yourself if you begin talkin' o' garden stuff, an' that like," said Mr. Swindell, sarcastically, " for I'll wager a trifle you'd make no scruples o' putting your currant-bushes into the ground with the sap up, an' the leaves on ; and I guess you can't tell whether Drumhead savoys come late or early, an' whether the Carter's champion brocolo, or the Dilcock's bride come afore the Purple-sproutin'; an' I'll warrant you can't tell the secret o' celery bein' holler an' pipey. I'm as good a man as you any day o' the week, an' I know my trade, an' have growd some good things for ole Gallopper at Castle House."

"Your part was on'y a poor one," said Boulder; "potterin' an' messin' about. You talk as if you made the lily out o' the mud with them hands. You might as well try to play snap-dragon with the stars."

" You're bent on quarrelin', curse you," said the gardener. " Have a care, my touch ain't like the thistle-down's. There's a sort o' flaver o' Gulley or Perrins in this fist, an' I ain't sure I couldn't spoil the look o' you, for I ain't so much at the time o' life when age begins to tell quick, an' I've some science o'

my side, an' that's everything. It's a lie that
' Choppin' Slack ' was a'most whopped by a
chaw-bacon, an' ' Dutch Sam ' by a butcher ;
but its true that Pearce thrashed three game-
keepers at once, an' Richmond punished a
couple of soldiers one after the other."

" If you lay a finger on me," said Boulder,
" I'll give that nose o' yourn a touch that 'ill
make it turn uppard like a hyana's, an' I
ain't sure that 'ont give you an expression fit
for such a concated chap. Don't you give
me any o' your threats, for, if I thought
proper, I'd tar an' feather you with these
hands afore twelve o'clock to-night. What's
the use o' you braggin' loud to me ? Haven't
I thrashed you before; an' haven't I seen
you at home under petticoat rule, an' haven't
I seen you carryin' home sticks an' stalks, an'
dried ole vegetables for fuel as a peace-
offerin', when you've been a little extry on
the spree ? Not that I blame a woman for

defendin' herself. A hen 'ill peck, an' a cow
'ill toss, so natur' meant the females to show
fight; but it don't add a sight to the dignity
of a bullyin' sort o' chap to be frightened by
a woman's tongue."

" I'm thinkin' she may be havin' a word
or two with you before you leave our house,
which I hope 'ill be soon," said Mr. Swindell.

" May-be she will," said Boulder; " not
that she want to make a piece o' work to
force me out o' the house. I've had enough
of it, though I ain't fond o' change. There
are more comfor'ble places to be had for
the payin', an' if it wasn't for the tobacco
I smoke the house would be a bit frousy."

" You'd better tell all this to my wife," said
Mr. Swindell, scornfully.

" If need be, I will, an' more too; for I'll
say that her talk have sometimes made me
think that ᴧole Harry ride on women's

tongues ; that that tongue of hers is sharp an' strong enough to make into the tooth of a rat-trap ; an' that if I'd such a mustard-pot, such a wasp of a wife, I'd be inclined to tie her to a linen-press with a bit o' chain cable, an' cram her mouth wi' cinders, or rags, or lobster-shells."

".Come, come, Mr. Boulder," said the landlord, " this is hard talk. Mrs. Swindell is a woman we all know that bear herself most respectable."

" It 'ud ha' bin a good thing for you if you'd had such a wife," said Swindell.

" Her money might ha' bin useful to me," said Boulder ; "but I don't think I could ha' put up with the ill-convenience for the sake o' the money, as I've heard you say you can do. Not that you touch a sight of it, for she keep a pretty tight hold on it. There's other ' nippers ' besides Mrs. Scrab Ash-bockin' in this here town. You don't want

to set about protestin' any more, Mr.
Mumbles, for I'm now off home. But I want
to ask this here Mr. Swindell if he's goin' to
offer me, myself, this here bet about my pays.
If he ain't, I'll take it the other way, an' offer
him a suvren agen that old hat of his, which
I'd hull on to the nearest muck-heap, that I
pay the money due for my son within six
month o' the time. You'll take that? Well
done. I'll win the bet. There ain't no pud-
dlin' about the offin' wi' me when I want to
go ashore. There ain't no play about me,
an' I don't sit soakin' an' laughin' here, night
after night. I ha'nt got no jokes an' smiles
to spare, an' them as have pay for 'em wi'
the glooms arterwards."

" The money must be got by fair means,
mind," said Mr. Swindell, sarcastically.
" None o' the old black tricks."

" Curse you!" exclaimed Boulder, angrily.
" They're all done with, an' forgotten."

"Don't you be so sure o' that," retorted the gardener. "They ain't so easy shook off. An' there be them as make mighty changes, but are yet too rotten at heart to die out o' their boots."

Boulder rose with an oath, but the landlord interposed.

"I 'ont have no rows here," he said firmly; "an' it's like this here, I call all here present to help me to keep the peace. Mr. Boulder, sir, be quiet, an' think o' poor Bedin'fel'. Keep a check on yourself, or go home; for you don't understan' the humours o' the place, an' the liquor have partlys got hold of you."

"Give me another six o' rum, an' go to the devil," said Boulder. "This here Swindell have insulted me; but I don't want no fightin' nor foul talk. If it wornt that I've mixed so long, and still hev to mix, with such a rough set, my son 'ud ha' made me partlys a gentleman by this time. I'll go quiet home to him. Give me nine o' rum, insteads o' six, an' keep that booby's tongue still in his hid. An' why don't one o' you sing us a song ? We used to have singin' a plenty in this here room. Come, a song, an' then I'll be trippin' my anchor for home."

After some hesitation, a quiet fisherman, called " Mute Tom Mockett," was persuaded to break forth into music, and sang a merry song. It was received with loud plaudits, to which the voice of Pilot Buzzard contributed conspicuously. Yet that singer's way was overshadowed with debt and difficulty, and that jocular Palinurus shortly afterwards went home to a consumptive wife, daily expecting death. But no one caught the bitter undertone in the laughter and in the song.

Boulder finished his rum, and then left the house. Before he reached home, however, he turned into the "Barge" for a supplementary libation.

As he entered Sunrise Lodge, Mrs. Swindell plunged into the little passage, expecting to confront her husband, with whom she was very indignant for his absence from home on the last night of their daughter's holiday. She, however, stepped back on seeing Boulder, for she always paid him a little respect.

"You've not seen my husband, I s'pose?" she said, withdrawing still further from her lodger, as she noticed, with surprise, suspicious signs of inebriation upon him.

"I've left him at the Lug-sail, ma'am," said Boulder thickly; "I dessay he'll be home afore midnight, but not in any good temper, ma'am."

"I don't want you nor yet anybody else to speak against him," said Mrs. Swindell, rather emboldened by the appearance of her daughter upon the scene. " But I call God to witness," she added, smoothing her dress impetuously, " that it's as bad as to spit on a parson as for a hulking, drinking man to spend his evening in a public-house full of beer and beastliness, and then to come home and be sulky with his sober wife, with a daughter there too, which a better girl don't want to be. But I'm sorry to find you've bin in such company."

" Didn't you never hear, ma'am, o' the old woman who wouldn't mind her own business ? She fell over a door-scraper an' broke her back."

" I don't want any sauce and rude talk from you."

" Nor yet I from you. I wish you was like a gad-fly, and hadn't any mouth at all," said Boulder.

At this instant George called to him from the sitting-room above, and he walked upstairs rather unsteadily. His son immediately detected his condition, and Boulder noticed a shadow of deep mortification in the young man's face.

" Father, this is terrible."

Boulder sat down.

" I ain't goin' to deny bein' sadly," he said, with a somewhat sheepish and sighing show of self-satisfaction at his own candour. "Am I one to deny truths? No. If so, may I never hev six foot o' groun' to be buried in, though, if it worn't for you, lad, I should like enough hev had a grave o' salt-water afore this. I've bin i' the wrong, I've played the fool with the liquor. I shipped too much at the Lug-sail, an' then some more at the Barge, but not a desp'rit heavy sea altogether. I'll put into port agin quick, if I can. They spoke agen me, boy, an' you, too, an' him as own this house was the wust of 'em. An' they made bets on me that I wouldn't carry out my plans about you, an' I made my bet, an' I'll win it."

"You'll do little good, father, by giving way like this," said George, in a very doleful voice. "You darken our prospects terribly."

"Breath o' my body!" cried Boulder. "I 'ont do no injury to you, but I'll win this bet, by Heaven!"

He had scarcely uttered these words when a heavy blow was struck on the front-door of the house, and when it was opened, a gruff voice was heard to ask: "Is Mr. Boulder above-stairs, ma'am?"

"It's Oby Smith," said the fisherman, moving clumsily to the door and opening it. "Let him roll up here, missis, an' get out the bottle o' Irish whisky, George. I 'ont take no more myself, lad; don't look so pitiful— but I feel as if one more glass 'ud do me good."

"It's foul news I've got," said Oby Smith,

a sturdy beachman, as he entered the room.

"Out with it man, an' put this glass o' whisky down your throat in its place. My boy 'ont let me have none."

The new comer stared for a moment at the unusually red face of the life-boat cockswain, drank his whisky, and continued :

" Ned Chapman has just swimmed ashore in the moon-light. He was out with Reuben Hole i' the little boat you know of watchin' nets, an' they were both eatin' a bit o' supper, an' they'd fastened the sheet to somethin', when down come a stiff puff o' wind sudden, and over she went ; an', as luck 'ud hev it, she filled, and went under water like a stone, an' poor Reuben's drownded."

Boulder sank down upon a seat, and stared wildly at the stuffed bittern for some instants. Then he said :

" Ain't there no trace o' the boat at all ?"

Oby shook his head.

"They put out directly, an' all as could be done was done."

"Go your ways, Oby," said Boulder, pointing to the door. "I'll be down on the beach in a twinkle. George, boy, come with me, though I feel more inclined to hide my hid under the bed-clothes. I lent poor Reuben, an honest man an' true, fifty pounds o' good money, an' the only security I'd got was the boat that's gone down. I'll lose my bet after all. Come on to the beach ; you must let me lean on your arm, though this news is a soberer, too."

But on the beach the old fisherman found no comfort but such as could be derived from the sympathetic glances of some who knew of his interest in the lost boat. George persuaded him to return home soon, and they parted for the night.

But shortly after midnight George Hern

was roused from his sleep by the sound of a footstep on the garden path, and going to his window he saw the form of his father disappear beneath the arch-way leading to Mr. Ashbocking's premises. Vividly remembering the excited state in which he had left Boulder at his bedroom-door, he at once resolved to follow him; and throwing on some of his clothes, dropped as noiselessly as possible from his window once more.

It was a beautiful night, and the solemn moonlight and a tender silver mist seemed to enchant the earth into a strange similitude with the sky. The wind came in sudden gusts that set the grove trees whispering with a sound like rain; but in the pauses of these gusts, there was a quivering, listening air on all things, and the faint moan of the sea was like the music of a dream.

Just as Hern passed through the archway, he saw his father's form on the edge of the corner bed which screened the window of Mrs. Oscar's lumber-room, and then disappear among the shrubs, which wore a fantastic look in the moon-light as the intruder pushed them asunder. He followed, and when he was near enough to peep through the greenery, he saw his father stooping down with his left hand buried in a tangled mass of wall-flowers and snowy petunia, narrowly examining this window, a little part of whose dingy face was glorified by the moon to the brightness of the jewelled palaces of fairy-land.

The son's next step reached the father's ear and he started with an oath, and turned round fiercely.

" Father, come home, what are you doing here ?"

" And what are you doin' here, George Hern? The old devil is in me, lad !"

" You are excited to-night ; rest will set you right. Come home."

" There's moneys there, boy, that 'ill never be missed, an' I've lost fifty pound to-night."

" Oh, father!"

The young man stepped back with a horrified, almost indignant look ; but the next instant he advanced, took his father's arm with the gentle touch of deep filial sympathy, which sent a thrill through the powerful man, and led him home.

CHAPTER VII.

I AM unwilling to meddle with the mass of
gossip which the rumour of the engagement
between George Hern and Miss Ashbocking
set on foot throughout Heathhammock, especially as on the third evening after that on
which Reuben Hole's boat was lost an event
occurred which furnished the public with
fresh material for talk and speculation.

On this evening Mr. and Mrs. Kidd
Ashbocking had arranged to call upon Mr.
and Mrs. Oscar, and the latter were seated,
with Clara, in the old blue drawing-room,
awaiting their arrival. The crisis in his
daughter's affairs reconciled the town-clerk to

this absence from his study, though he had left unfinished, on the previous evening, a list of passages from Solon and from Nehemiah, between which he had hoped to find more subtle points of agreement than had yet been noticed.

Clara seemed calm, but a close observer would have marked many traces of anxiety and lack of peace in her face. Mrs. Oscar was very pale and stern and silent.

Mr. Oscar made a few remarks on matters of local interest, but he could hardly have engaged the sympathies of his audience less if he had spoken of the quietism of Moline or the nominalism of Occam. Gloom pre-vailed.

After a short time, however, Mrs. Oscar left the room, and then Clara looked up from her work and said :

" My mother is not well, I am afraid."

" She is certainly not well," replied her

father, "and her temper, you see, is not very agreeable. Like Philip, the son of Demetrius, she is much oppressed with sleeplessness."

"I am beginning to feel some of my troubles pressing hard upon me. But I shall not fall under them."

"I am glad you have consented to go away for a time. I am not very familiar with affairs of the heart; but your mother approves of this visit, and I approve of her recommendations."

"I will gladly consent to anything that you and my mother suggest, if it does not absolutely clash with my one cherished project. I am sorry she takes this project so much to heart; but I am thankful, father, that you think less gravely of it."

Mr. Oscar drew his chair nearer to her.

"Yet it is my duty to think gravely of it," he said. "But I will tell you a secret," he added, in a low voice. "A discovery which I (penetrating, as it were, into the character of your mother) have made. Your mother for a long time has been haunted by a sort of dread that the somewhat strong ingredient of severity in her composition may have just a little lessened and discouraged the love she earnestly wishes to gain from you ; and she looks upon the occurrences of the last few days as grimly confirmatory of her fears."

"Ah, I will not have her pained by such a thought, though I confess, father—but you can guess what I would say. Let it pass, for you and I have been taught by long experience that there is the sterling inner affection under the outward frown, even when it is most unlovely."

"Yes, yes, indeed," said Mr. Oscar warmly.

"I can only hope the day will come," said Clara, with a sigh, "when I can reconcile her to my marriage, and when you will unreluctantly forgive me."

"'Forgive!' the word sounds strangely to me. I hope I am not malicious and unforgiving, though Walpole says the race is pestilently bad and malevolent. Brasidas, however, was inclined to assign revenge to the most contemptible. I strive to look hopefully on the future, my dear. I don't waste time with vain regrets—lamenting, for instance, that George Hern did not go to the wars and perish, like Masistius, in a charge of cavalry——"

He drew back his chair hastily, for Mrs. Oscar returned to the room at this moment.

"We shall have to be thinking about your wardrobe, child," she said after a solemn pause. "Where did you get those new gloves that lie upon your dressing-table?"

"I bought them of Mr. Beamish."

"Rather unsubstantial things ; but I have never said to you, as my grandmother used to say to my mother, 'Dress as I like, or keep in bed.' Perhaps I should have been wiser if I had ruled you with a firmer hand ; for you certainly were sometimes a troublesome child."

"Not very, I think," said Mr. Oscar ; "though you occasionally showed passion when, after a term of idleness, you figured poorly at my little examinations and I had to report the fact truthfully to you."

"You should have aimed at getting serviceable gloves," said Mrs. Oscar.

"Don'tyou think these will last long?"asked Clara, with a rather weary turn of her head.

"No ; they will last about as short a time as your share of pocket-money has always done."

"And yet you wish sometimes to reduce that," said Clara, with a slight smile. "Such a proceeding would be like asking a beggar for change out of a half-penny you have given him."

" Ah, child," said Mrs. Oscar, with an icy glance, "let us hope the time will never come when you will be glad to receive a packet of rush-lights for a present."

" Let us hope so, indeed," said Clara, smiling again.

" Yes, but let us not be too confident on the point. There is no telling to what pass Miss Ashbocking may not be brought down, when she is Mrs. George Hern. I heartily wish we had never heard of George Hern——"

Clara's eyes brightened as she looked at her mother now, for the latter's tone was sharp and hard.

" Do not speak against him, mother," she exclaimed, calmly but firmly. " I am here, and ready to receive your censure. I think I shall never sink to so distressing a position as that you seem to hint at. I am not alarmed by any forebodings of great poverty. The loss of position I will try to face with- out a sigh, though perhaps I may sometimes fail a little. I shall be far, far happier married to the man I love, though he was born in a workhouse, than I could be if married to one unable to touch my heart, though he could boast as proud a motto as the Grantleys or the Templetowns."

" When one once begins to lower one's self," said Mrs. Oscar, " it is easy to keep descend- ing, I should say. When once one deli- berately turns aside from a good, promising, prosperous course——"

" I prefer the perilous course I have chosen," said Clara firmly ; "and I could not settle down in any other. The course you take suits you, mother."

" And would suit you, as you may one day, when it is too late, most bitterly acknowledge," said Mrs. Oscar, shuffling her feet impatiently.

" I think not. Mother, there is something better than mere prudence and caution."

"Something that looks better to a foolish girl, but is in reality a quagmire and a snare."

" Your rules would make life a dreary term indeed; and what is the end? We must drop every loaf and fish before we step into Charon's boat, nor will he let the most accomplished haggler and chafferer bargain for the most comfortable seat."

" You are a brave girl, Clara," said Mr. Oscar; " and I believe you intend to be, and are not unlikely to prove, a very Arria to your Pœtus. But your mother gives her counsel in all affection."

" Yes, yes," said Clara, " and we will not quarrel. But, mother, you must try to speak more kindly to me. I know your heart is not a cold or a dwarfish one, and I know that I am indeed an object of great interest to it. You will not disgrace your sex by refusing to be kind," she added, advancing to Mrs. Oscar, and taking her hand. "There! you have cleared some of the cloud from your face. I don't intend to lose my power over you in all my troubles. I believe I could induce you to give me a sovereign now if I wished, in spite of my carelessness with my pocket-money."

"I positively believe," exclaimed Mr. Oscar, merrily, "that there may be, among other charms in those bright eyes, some money-getting witchery."

"You talk foolishly," said Mrs. Oscar, shaking her head, though she could not hide a half smile that could be traced more clearly in the eyes than on the lips. "She may make her eyes shine like crystal, but they can't draw money from a wise woman without some prudent claim to back them."

" Then you might dim these eyes with tears," said Clara, with a rather melancholy attempt at merriment.

" And some eyes look the better for a little water. I should form my own opinion as to the reasonableness of the tears. Remember, you are dealing with a strong-minded personage."

The conversation was stopped by the entrance of Trippington, who turned her face towards her mistress, and with downcast eyes, which she had scarcely dared to raise during the last few days, announced, " Mr. and Mrs. Kidd Ashbocking, ma'am."

Mrs. Kidd wore a jacket of black beaver cloth, liberally trimmed with plush—a rich gold-shaded dress, and a bonnet, whose predominant green hues matched her florid complexion but poorly. Mr. Kidd was perhaps a little more neatly attired than usual—no small admission when one knows that about ten minutes before he had bustled from among his prickly pears, melon-thistles, and night-flowering cacti, much soiled at knee and elbow, and holding in hands, like a tinker's in colour, a favourite toad, a flower-pot, a bit of window-lead, and a packet of tobacco-seed.

His face looked rather careworn as he took a seat against the wall under a stuffed loris, a time-honoured but rather incongruous occupant of the old blue drawing-room. Mrs. Kidd's eyes were rather red, and her voice was not very cheerful.

" It's quite a treat to get my husband out for a visit," she said. " Early and late he's busy, and worrying about something. I don't want to interfere, but I believe he takes less rest than any man in Heathham-mock."

"I claim for my husband that he does more good, sound, lucrative business than any man in Heathhammock," said Mrs. Oscar drily, and turning to her daughter.

Clara had previously received a hint that the discussion between the seniors this evening would be of a private character; so, after listening to a short argument between her father and Mr. Kidd as to the wisdom of the civil law (according to Puffendorf), and the law of England, in not recognising bees as "feræ naturæ," she withdrew.

Mrs. Oscar, who had clearly foreseen the object of her guests' visit, led up to it by a few direct remarks. She then said—

"The Admiral and I do not often agree; but I confess (not that I wish to speak incautiously, and not that I have yet formed my opinion of your son) that many another match might have satisfied me less; and I speak for my husband also."

" And to have the match put off in such a way, and by such a young man as this Hern !" said Mrs. Kidd, raising her eyebrows.

" It is not put off yet, though we deal with no trifler in Clara," said Mrs. Oscar. " In firmness, as in many other qualities, she is far above most girls."

" She's a loveable creature," said Mrs. Kidd. " But it is such a pity she has to go away just as Storker returns. And he begins to like her, I'm sure ; for he said only this morning that, though she's decidedly a fine girl, her touch is as light as a falling leaf's. But now we shall have no chance of bringing the young people together."

" That would be a profitless experiment, I think," said Mr. Oscar, mildly.

" It might and should be tried," rejoined his wife.

" The Admiral has suggested——" began Mr. Kidd.

" And you musn't mind agreeing with the Admiral in this matter, Mary Ann," said Mrs. Kidd; "for, I assure you, he has taken a very great interest in these young people; and he is not fond of young people generally, especially children. I never saw him much more irritable than on the evening that Kidd had some of the school children to tea at Castle House, and amused them with a magic lantern. The Howsegoes, he says, were never fond of children; but I'm fond of them, and that's the truth. I've heard him say, too, that a delicate wine pays better for careful nursing than a delicate child."

" No doubt he is glad that you have not six or seven Storkers," said Mrs. Oscar.

" And perhaps you are too, Mary Ann; for I've heard you say I talk too much about the one I have."

" Mothers are generally apt to err in this respect," said Mr. Kidd.

" Especially the weaker-minded," muttered Mrs. Oscar.

" The Admiral would seem to approve of the old pagan custom, referred to by Herodotus," interposed Mr. Oscar, "of wearing mourning at a birth."

" We are wandering from the point," said Mrs. Oscar. " What is it that the Admiral suggests ?"

" That we should have a dinner-party at once," said Mr. Kidd, " which will give the young people one good opportunity of meeting, to begin with."

" I am glad you take some interest in the matter, Kidd," said Mrs. Oscar. "When George Hern is discussed, one would think my conservative husband a more advanced liberal than you, a perfect ' leveller.' "

"So far as concerns the keeping of young men like Hern in their proper places," said Mr. Kidd, "I am wholly and fully conservative."

"Ah, you must not give me cause to nickname you, like Theramenes," said Mr. Oscar, smiling.

"I think it's a pity that George Hern's father did not 'give him a trade,' as they say," said Mrs. Kidd; "and then he might have 'kept an acquaintance' in his own circle. But what do you think of the dinner-party, Mary Ann? Papa says it is to be a really good one. My dinners have not always been altogether successful, as you know; nor, indeed, have other people's; for when we dined at Mrs. Pittock's, in the Christmas week, just after her new cook came, the Admiral was very much annoyed with the dinner. It was terrible to hear his stiff shirt creak. I shall never forget it."

"He is too fond of looking at the wrong side of things," said Mrs. Oscar.

"He is worse than Ariel about good food," said Mrs. Kidd; "for though Ariel looks rather disdainfully at poor bits, he doesn't often altogether decline them. But I shall never forget Mrs. Pittock's dinner. The turkey was a large, sinewy bird, and the mutton cutlets, as papa said, had been turned about twice in five times the number of minutes; and the suet in the plum-pudding, as Kidd said, made its presence known most presumptuously. And then, Mrs. Pittock's little grandson, Paul, who was not dainty, wanted more of the pudding than he could have, and made a groaning and sniffing most grievous to be borne. And, to make matters worse, the cook was out of temper, and the clattering that came from the kitchen made Mrs. Pittock's face as red as the boy's. But I think I can turn out a dinner properly."

"A very strong mind is not essential to the performance of this trivial item of a female's duties," said Mrs. Oscar, tartly.

"At any rate, I shall not be so anxious about my servants as I should be if I had your Trippington," said Mrs. Kidd; "for I sometimes think you might puzzle her if you asked her suddenly the number of her fingers. I can get help, if I like, from the 'Hanging Sword;' but I can bustle about myself, though less active than I used to be, and rather large—not that I regret that, for many reasons; for, as Storker says, I ought to take it as a blessing that I can peep at the world's doings above the heads of the people about me : and that I can generally do, be they many or few. Well, if we have this dinner-party, I will set about it systematically."

"And light the gas early in the evening, as you did when the Rajah Cooch Krishna's kinsman visited Heathhammock, and did us the honour to dine with us," said Mr. Kidd, with a smile, " in order that the room might be well filled with *light* when the company came."

" I dislike expensive dinner-parties," said Mrs. Oscar ; " when one must have mock-turtle instead of gravy soup, and hock instead of good mild ale. However, you must please yourselves ; and, at any rate, I would rather that you acted as host, Bella, than myself, though, perhaps, I could come nearer to the exactitude of a French housewife in the adjustment of my dishes. I pay so high a price for coals, that extensive cooking preparations would be anything but agreeable to me."

"What are you burning now, Mary Ann?" asked Mr. Kidd. " I am interested in this subject, as I burn not a few coals among the coke for my forcing houses."

" Some black sea-borne stuff I bought of
Skipper Eeles. I hope it's coal, but cannot
tell. But why," she added severely, " do we
keep wandering from the point ?"

Mr. Kidd moved timidly in his chair, and
Mr. Oscar said—

" Mary Ann is not quite well this evening,
as perhaps you may have noticed."

" I noticed it," said Mrs. Kidd, " although
I didn't like to say anything ; for I know she
doesn't like remarks of that kind. I wish
she would see Dr. Staggold. I was with
him not three hours ago, and we were
talking about the effect of digitalis on the
heart."

" Suppose we talk of the matter in hand
now," said Mrs. Oscar. " I raise no objection to the bringing of our young people
together in the way you suggest. I don't
approve of these bringings together in the
abstract, however ; and in Mr. Audrey's and

Mr. Ormerod's cases my husband and I had no occasion to interfere at all. I certainly don't approve of hurrying young persons into matrimony."

" It is difficult to say who are young persons in these times," said Mrs. Kidd; "and as to childhood, the boys seem to sprout up into men in a year or two, and so do the girls."

" I object to early marriages," continued Mrs. Oscar. " Surely it is not pleasant for a father to hear his son say, ' My father and I were boys together.' Besides, a family springs up, and leans for support upon parents who have not strengthened and seasoned themselves with a fair struggle with the world. Liabilities crowd in before any store is laid up to meet them, and anxieties follow, ending perhaps in loss of heart and a blighted life ; and your young hopeful sinks into a ruined man, who mustn't be too proud to touch his hat to those who were at one time his inferiors."

"Well," said Mrs. Kidd, "Storker says that before he went to America, he knew no more about life than a cat about clinical surgery."

"Travel is a good instructor," said Mr. Oscar, "but as Kitto observes, in order to travel usefully one must carry information with him, and the information obtained will be in exact proportion to the information carried. Our rather unambitious friend Storker would have profited far more by his trip if he had been more of a reading man. When I was but a little older than he is now, I had much of the enthusiasm of a Bunsen or a Haydn. I was as fond of the bookshelves as Archimedes or Csoma de Körös. I would have retired to them from the presence of a king, as Marmier tells us Goethe did to his 'Faust.' I am like Seneca, an advocate for the cultivation of the mind. It is culture that raises a man so far above another of equal intellect."

"Perhaps you are drawing a comparison between yourself and me," said Mr. Kidd, mildly, for his cousin had turned to him. "I will not contradict you, though I cannot agree that information is only acquired by the reading man. But you know my views. Hundreds of books are in my opinion little better than mere words and moonshine."

"There is no book but may prove a door to a range of stirring thoughts," said Mr. Oscar. "There is no book on all my shelves, no little book in Dr. Staggold's nursery, or in the most primitive of ragged-schools, but may be rightly labelled 'history.'"

"And the best of chronicles called histories," said Mr. Kidd, "are yet as different from the history of a living heart as a moss rose from a star."

" There is a flavour of truth in that," said Mr. Oscar, frankly.

" The mass of book-lore is stupendous," said Mr. Kidd ; "but I think its practical utility is utterly inadequate. It is true, I refer with satisfaction to such works as Tooke's ' History of Prices,' or ' White's ' Cattle Medicine,' or Markham's book on ' Farriery,' or Kollar's on ' Injurious Insects.' "

" You will never agree on these things," said Mrs. Oscar.

" Talking of the utility of book-lore," said Mr. Oscar, "my reading enabled me once (though conscious of much change in money-value) to gratify our rather discontented curate by telling him that, at one time, an English bishop paid his chaplain three half-pence a day, a lower remuneration than that of Roger Fylpott, learned in the law, who received three-and-eightpence for his counsel

and fourpence for his dinner, or than that of
the Athenian senators, according to Thucy-
dides, who were paid a drachma or six oboli,
that is, sevenpence-three-farthings per diem.
I think, too, one might somewhat console
a poor man who is complaining of the hard-
ness of his lot, by giving him some details
of the miseries which the subjects of mighty
tyrants have undergone, or even by telling him
that workmen's wages in the time of Aris-
tophanes were fourpence-halfpenny a day."

"Storker certainly takes after me, Oscar,
in not being fond of books," said Mrs. Kidd,
"for I never could read long. Storker says
that I would rather eat poached game than
go through the brown book of Hume's
'Essays ;' and, though I suppose I ought not
to encourage poaching, I really think I
would. But he doesn't take after me in
being fond of church-work, nor yet in singing
and liking music. He says I would almost

submit to the bite of the tarantula for the sake of the music afterwards."

"Music has played an important part in the world," said Mr. Oscar. "Evius was not the only musician who has received honours, nor Philoxenes the only one who has been oppressed."

"If Storker, though an inmate of Castle House, becomes a punctual and diligent man of business, he will have no occasion to regret his lack of musical taste," said Mr. Oscar.

"Many have successfully combined music with their pursuits before and since the days of Thersander," said Mrs. Oscar.

"Storker will never combine it with anything," said Mrs. Kidd. "He says he has less music in him than the mollusk has blood ; like Kidd, he prefers the simplest ballad to the best operatic airs. He will sometimes listen to me if I sing such a piece as 'I would I were a bird.'"

" That is a foolish song," interposed Mrs. Oscar, gruffly. " You would hardly choose to be a bird altogether, whatever share of faculties Providence has given you ; and if you only obtained the bird's capacity of flying, your wings would craze your dressmaker. But we are once more wandering from the point."

" I was thinking," said Mr. Kidd, "that we had only dealt with one-half of the subject which we came here to discuss. Should Storker and Clara become man and wife, I have determined to make some considerable improvements in Castle House, and to hand it over to them. Should your daughter ever become my son's wife, Mary Ann, he shall take her to a home worthy of her."

Mrs. Oscar's face brightened a little, but she said curtly :

" I should have thought that the house was already in a very tolerable plight."

"Time has told its tale upon many parts. It can and shall be improved," said Mr. Kidd. "I shall rather enjoy the work ; and I consider myself a fit person to undertake it. Will you not acknowledge that, Oscar ?"

"Your heart will be in it I think," said the town-clerk, smiling.

"Yes," said Mrs. Kidd. "Storker says he would willingly pass a few years fastened into the old stocks on Church Green, in order to study their structure, if his friends asked him to build some."

"I expect, Kidd," said Mr. Oscar, "that I could puzzle you with a question or two on Beckford's architectural or Shenstone's horticultural ideas ; but you are a practical man."

"I've heard him say he believed he could make a watch, after a time, with his own hands," said the banker's wife."

"And yet his sight is poor," said Mr. Oscar. "His eyes are by no means like those of Draco, the son of Eupompus. But, Kidd, I never wish to underrate practical work."

" I would rather concern myself with a scheme for utilising boats as carriages after the boating season," said Mr. Kidd, " than with speculations whether there is any like-lihood of our becoming monkeys after death."

" I will not underrate practical work," con-tinued Mr. Oscar, " nor sneer at those who, like Paulus Ægineta, take pleasure in testing the conclusions of the theorists. I really believe, Kidd, that you understand much of the practical work of the builder."

" But you must remember," said Mrs. Oscar, " that the boiler you built in one of your forcing houses burst, because you dis-regarded the hints of other practical men."

" That was unfortunate, I grant," said Mr. Kidd, with a shrug. " But while I was

groping about after the remains of the boiler,
I had the satisfaction of discovering that the
bed just outside the forcing-house produced
the best red worms (for bait) I ever met
with. I don't often miscarry in my practical plans ; and I have pretty accurate ideas
about buildings, from those as strong as
London Bridge to those as frail as a specu-
lative builder's cottages."

" No one could have better adjusted the
sash in my office-window, which extreme age
had reduced to creaking and quivering im-
becility," said Mr. Oscar.

" He's a wonder with windows," said Mrs.
Kidd. " I sometimes think he should have
been a glazier."

" I could, no doubt, have earned a fair
living," said Mr. Kidd, complacently ; "but
a glazier's is only a half-year's trade. By
the way, Mary Ann, I have for some time
intended to remind you that you should have

a little coal-tar put on the troughs at the
back of your house. That is a job I can't
quite undertake myself."

"We could hardly expect it, if you are
going to set about extensive alterations at
Castle House," said Mr. Oscar. "I won't
ask you to reveal your plans; for I know you
are not a great talker, and, doubtless, like
Werter, carry many unexpressed conceptions
in your mind."

"I hope something will be done to the
cellars," said Mrs. Kidd, "or we shall have
the rats about us, as they came about my
grandmother, eating into a Stilton cheese,
from below, so that nothing was left but the
hollow rind; and you could wear it on your
head like a hat."

"The cellar shall certainly be looked to,"
said Mr. Kidd, readily; "and I propose
an extra passage. A passage, you know,
is always a convenience, and, in a cottage,

generally adds £2 per annum to the rental. But the passage, in my case, is not the most significant point."

"And there is the garden to improve," said Mrs. Kidd, " which will be more in my way; for gardening is more woman's work. I often think it probable that Adam attended to the wild beasts in Eden and Eve to the flowers, but I don't know. I'm fond of my flowers, but can't take much interest in vegetables, though papa does. He says to me, 'Give your best thoughts to what can be brought to table, if it be only borrage, which makes " cool tankard." ' I know you are careful with your vegetables, Mary Ann. Did your papa——"

" I always called him 'father,' " said Mrs. Oscar, drily.

"Yes, I should remember that, for Clara calls Oscar so."

" Let us return to the building question,"

said the other lady, "if there is any more to say."

Some little talk ensued about bricks and studs, battens, poles, putlogs, orangeries, smoking temples, dormer windows, fillets and quirks, and other items of a like nature, and Mr. Oscar favoured (or tortured) his audience with allusions to the figures at the portal of the Khorsabad Palace in Nineveh ; the subterranean drainworks of Bœotia ; the elder-thatched, wicker-walled church of Glastonbury; the grand old porch at Esneh ; Ctesiphon's temple, and Coudray's architectural performances ; and with references to the works of Grunder, Perrouet, Hutton, and Vitruvius, and a short quotation from Lamb's "Studies of Ancient Domestic Architecture."

"Isn't it all wonderful ?" said Mrs. Kidd. " I can't follow so much learned conversation, but no doubt the fault is with my own apprehension ; for, as Storker once said, when I could not understand some great scheme of his father's, ' A flea may look upon a pretty baby as a very cumbrous lout.' I hope you'll be satisfied with these alterations when they're done, Mary Ann."

" I hope so," said Mrs. Oscar. " You have the Admiral at your back and inclined to be liberal (and I must confess I rather admire the extreme care he has taken of his money) ; but count the cost ; for builders, besides disarranging your place in a manner quite intolerable to such a lover of order as myself, are said by some to be little better than felons. Certainly, in contract work, the extras are sometimes so gross, that your original price for a house will hardly pay for the ground-floor rooms."

" There's not much fear of imposition to one who can tell the number of bricks in a wall as quickly as the builder himself," said

Mr. Kidd, with a self-satisfied smile. " I am not a man who would build a house and leave no hole for the staircase, or design a mid-sea lighthouse with trellis-work outside for vines."

" You may think the going into a smaller house is not very agreeable to me," said Mrs. Kidd; "nor is it. But they tell me it is all for the best, and I don't wish to interfere. Besides, I shall be a Howsegoe still : nothing can unmake me ; and when I die, I should like to be buried in the Howsegoe tomb at Wilford. It's pleasant to think one can be 'gathered unto one's own people.' Moreover, though I move into a small house, I shall be able to continue my church-work and no doubt grow flowers."

" And wear gay colours and present them to the public gaze," said Mrs. Oscar, rather impatiently.

" Oh yes," replied the good-natured lady

of Castle House, "and no doubt we shall find a comfortable little place, and one not too small, like some friend of papa's who had to sleep in the parlour and keep his liquors in the linen-closet. But we must be going home, Kidd. I am sorry to see you looking so poorly, Mary Ann. I hope you will be better when next we meet."

" You have brightened her up a little this evening," said Mrs. Oscar, "and I am glad of it. Nothing should make us melancholy to excess. The philosopher does not look on life with lowered brow ; and groans and grumblings mar the true tones of the world. The pictures of bitter, repulsive distress in such works as Voltaire's ' Œdipe' are not true reflections of life."

" I really wish you would see the doctor if not better to-morrow," said Mrs. Kidd, as she took Mrs. Oscar's hand.

" No," said Mrs. Oscar firmly, " I won't

have him try experiments upon me with his pills and his setons and his diluents and I know not what. It's fortunate he's not such an experimentalist as Kidd, or the grave-yard would be full very soon."

"Medical men," said Mr. Oscar, "should not limit their ambition to the range of accomplishments boasted by Boerhaave——"

But the town-clerk's wife was already weary of this long interview, and at this juncture contrived to usher her guests from the room.

When these latter reached Castle House and entered the drawing-room, they found the Admiral lying upon the sofa asleep ; so, fearing that disturbance might enrage him, they closed the door upon him and his companion Ariel, and seated themselves in the dining-room.

Storker soon afterwards strolled in, smoking the stump of a cigar. He had spent the evening at the Hanging Sword, where he had been playing at billiards and trying to buy of the landlord a fine fox-terrier as a companion for Moloch.

"It's grog-time," he said, after he had finished his cigar. "and we must summon the ancient to take his share. He sleeps so deeply at night that the most awful dream wouldn't wake him; and we don't often catch him napping in the evening. He mustn't be unsociable, hiding away like a bat in a cave. We must bring him out into the light and look at him."

He rose and walked into the drawing-room and advanced to the sofa there. He looked at the sleeper's neat blue coat, unbuttoned, as indeed it needed to be if real comfort were expected, and then at his bulbous nose and creased face, which the dim light seemed to becalm and to rob of its rubicund hue.

" There's not much trace of alert machinery

behind that still aulæum," whispered Storker, " and yet he has bestirred himself some little recently. Come, ancient," he added, raising his voice, " grog-time."

There was no answer, so the young man shook the sleeper's arm, but still no answer came.

Then Storker noticed that the spaniel seated close to the prostrate form was gazing at it with arching neck and suspicious eye, as he was wont, in winter, to gaze at the falling cinders from his post upon the hearth-rug.

He touched his grandfather's forehead and found it cold. He instantly started back, knocking from a little table close at hand the head of a Spanish battleaxe, a voyding knife, and a Phœnician medal, and called aloud his father; for he knew that Admiral Howsegoe's sleep was the deep sleep of death.

CHAPTER VIII.

THE coroner and his jury held an inquest over the remains of Admiral Howsegoe, and a verdict of "Death from natural causes" was returned. Apoplexy was the fatal disorder. Worry of mind and unchecked habits of gluttony, it was said, had caused a pressure of blood upon a brain already slightly injured by a head-wound.

The body was placed in the Howsegoe vault at Wilford, and the funeral was conducted with not a little ceremony, in accordance with the wishes of the Admiral's daughter. Hers, however, was the only eye in Heathhammock which showed a genuine

moisture that day, though I think that Mrs.
Pattock sighed rather grievously behind her
Venetian blind. The bearers, put into ill
humour by the great weight of the coffin,
were liberally regaled. Mr. Swindell, one of
them, went home at night helplessly drunk,
though comfortably conscious that his wife's
reproaches would be moderate, as he had been
tippling at the expense of the Kidd Ashbockings; and Peggy Nunn, the charwoman, who
had invited herself to spend this solemn
day with the servants at Castle House, was
ushered from it by Mr. Bilge in sore disgrace,
having thrown some hot punch into the face of
the cook at the close of an angry argument.

Much as Heathhammock found to talk
about in the sudden death of the dapper,
choleric old seaman, it found a still more
pregnant topic in the ugly rumour afloat the
day after the funeral, that he was not one
half so wealthy as had been supposed ; which

rumour grew gradually more inauspicious, as the day wore on, till it was reported far and wide that the Admiral had died a penniless man.

This was indeed true ; this was the revelation of the mysterious revered green box in the dressing room, which was forced on this day. Admiral Howsegoe had lost every shilling of his fine property in one vast foolish speculation, a project for importing Indian resin and manufacturing therefrom a varnish that should supersede all others ; and even his pension, save a few pounds of it allowed him for his wardrobe, was handed to a creditor as soon as received. This stolid, heavy - browed old gentleman had brain enough to play the hypocrite with much success. Seldom was deception more complete.

It is not to be wondered at that he felt so much anxiety to secure Clara Ashbocking and her money for the grandson he knew he must one day cruelly disappoint, and to insure for himself a comfortable home at Castle House, which, owing to his forebodings as to the state of his son-in-law's finances, seemed to him to be placed in jeopardy.

He had at times cunningly dropped hints, here and there, that he intended to benefit Heathhammock by his will, but neither the corporate funds nor the pockets of the tradesmen from whose stores he used to perpetrate little thefts, were enriched by the value of a halfpenny.

The discovery of the disastrous truth did not break the heart of poor Mr. Kidd Ashbocking—nothing was likely to do that—but his face wore a gloomier shade on the day after the funeral than had ever been seen on it before. And, although he set about his customary work in the garden, and walked as usual to the sailors' reading-room to look through the large telescope there at the sea and to give a shilling to an old salt-water *protégé* of his, he avoided the bank altogether.

As to Mrs. Kidd, a very piteous little picture of wounded pride might be presented here ; but I will pass it by.

The afternoon post brought a letter from the Stock Exchange personage whose acquaintance the Admiral appeared to have made on Cannon Green, Heathhammmock, but who was, in reality, a friend of long standing. This correspondent, and he only, had been fully in the confidence of the deceased, and he threw some light upon his secret proceedings ; adding, that he was himself a creditor for a large loan advanced at a critical time, and that he trusted to the honour of the friends of Admiral Howsegoe for the discharge of his claim.

Mr. Kidd dropped the letter with a deep sigh.

" It is wholly and fully out of the question," he said, wiping his spectacles with a hand that trembled slightly. " Storker, my boy," he added, to his son, who had not been to the office that day, "get me a little brandy, and help yourself to some."

" We have both partaken pretty freely of port, sir," said Storker, whose complexion justified the remark, " but I'll join you ; what says that letter ?"

He took it up and read it.

" We must face the facts as they are," said Mr. Kidd. " I have relied upon your grand-father's help, and it has failed me. I should have handed over to you an embarrassed business, which I thought his capital would have cleared, but I am bound to confess that without his capital the embarrassment wears a very serious aspect. Moreover—to reveal a secret—I lent him, some two years ago, five thousand, for an investment of which he declined to give me particulars, though he paid the interest by some mysterious means."

"Oh, dear, dear!" said Mrs. Kidd, who was reclining on the sofa; "more and more trouble! What are we—what is the world coming to?"

"Is your business then in a "really precarious condition?" asked Storker, anxiously.

"The truth is simply this," said his father, with a grim effort at stoicism, " I must close the bank."

"The deuce you must!" cried Storker, with a muttered oath.

"Good gracious!" cried Mrs. Kidd, bursting into tears, "what shall we do? Is this the end of papa's great schemes for Storker? Ah! he sometimes led me to think you might get into trouble without his help, Kidd. But where is his help?"

"Where, indeed !" said Storker. " He used to say that he could manage things so much better than my father, and was fond of setting down as fools all who did not agree with him. But he has made a wreck of his own affairs — has not even carried out his promise of paying my travelling expenses to America, and has left nothing behind him but his wardrobe. The tailors here used to growl at him for having his clothes made in town ; they may now congratulate themselves that their books contain no unsettled items under his name. By George, how prodigiously well he has hoodwinked us. No wonder his sympathies with my early settlement in life seemed rather poignant. He had a good store of cunning in him, poor old gentleman, though I fear little else of greater value than a rag and bone merchant's store."

" I always thought him rather wise," said Mrs. Kidd, sorrowfully ; "and he thought he

was himself. He used to get very angry if
any one didn't listen to him. 'Am I a stuffed
monkey,' he used to say, ' only fit to turn
your back upon ?' But what are we to do in
our trouble, Kidd? Close the bank, indeed !"

" I must do that unless Oscar can make
a better arrangement."

" He will help you. Go to him."

" Yes, I must, of course, go to him !"

" We could enlist his sympathy and help,"
said Storker ; "but we can't tackle him without confronting his briar of a wife. He's like
a wood-worm in the roof, difficult to get at
without bringing something else about your
ears. But beggars mustn't be choosers : and
I suppose we might hurt ourselves by quarrelling with her. It isn't wise to imitate the
ichneumon in jumping down the crocodile's
throat."

" You and I will go to Oscar and Mary

Ann this evening, Bella," said Mr. Kidd; "and, meanwhile, Storker can help me to draw out a short statement of my affairs for their perusal. I have been shaping the main outlines in my mind this unhappy day."

" A sorry task for your son and heir, who little expected to find himself without a shekel, without the value of a poppy-head," said Storker, grimly. " And the statement will be a complicated one, too, I doubt. I'd rather copy out a nursery rhyme three hundred times. Hang it, my spirit is not disposed, as a rule, to prefigure the dolo-rous ; but this sort of calamity takes a stupendous discount off one's complacency."

" Let us hope the severe experience may prove of some profit, Storker," said Mr. Kidd, taking a draught of brandy and water.

" I have no more desire to test it, sir," said Storker, following his example, " than a countess might have to try a ride in a tumbril. One hardly cares to take a dog's bite in order to know what strength there is in his jaws. Where in the world has your money gone, sir ?"

"Your father has always been too kind," said Mrs. Kidd; " not that I wish to interfere, or to blame kindness. They say good acts bring their own reward ; but in his case, where is the reward ? As poor papa used to say——"

" I think we won't refer to him again just at present, mother," said Storker. " Let the ancient rest in peace. No wonder he broke down, with such a weighted conscience within his waistcoat. It galls me to think how he, too, often repaid you for your fleshpots and toothsome junkets with frowns and surly words. But I won't speak against the last of the Howsegoes, mother. You will be as heavy a sufferer as any of us. You would as willingly wear Glauce's gown as a shabby one, and can hardly dispense with your rings so well as Saturn could with his."

"I don't like the thought of poverty, I assure you," said Mrs. Kidd, mournfully; "but I suppose we are all fitted to our places somehow. One comfort is, my conscience doesn't blame me, though I may have muddled a little sometimes."

"No doubt you have not been so systematic a housekeeper as Mrs. Oscar," said Storker. "Why, ma'am, I should be no more astonished to hear London street-cries in a country lane, than to hear you cheapening shop-wares."

"I am sorry that this shadow should fall upon you, Bella," said Mr. Kidd, "for I know you like the bright side of life (except in the matter of your own ailments), and would gladly see more smiles, more gentleness, more friendship and beneficence."

"I hope I shan't be much humbled," she

exclaimed, " so that every common person will be as a brother or sister to me, and I have to look in vain for the civil salutations that even the most surly used to give me. And what about the bill I owe Miss Craggy and many others ? Shall I have to sell my dresses and things, and that little nainzook embroidery baby-frock of Storker's, which I have stored up these many years ? And what's to become of poor dear Ariel, and my church-work, and my music and flowers ? All seem blighted, and really I don't wonder at my having been ill for so long, with this hanging over me."

Mr. Kidd rubbed his bald head with his handkerchief, and looked very unhappy.

" I am afraid a bad time is coming to your curiosities, father," said Storker. " It would have been better if you had contented your-self with talking about polychromy, impasto, etc., like Mr. Oscar, instead of laying out so much money in pictures. And now, perhaps, your ivory Cupid and your cup of Syrian garnet, your silver bottle-waggon and your Crown Derby tazzas will be sold for a small fraction of the price you gave for them."

" Connoisseurs will come down to the sale, if any," said Mr. Kidd, rather bitterly.

" I should hope so," said Storker ; " for you might as well offer a palace for sale to paupers as your treasures to the burgesses of Heath-hammock."

" I have certainly not found a formidable rival in taste in the place," said Mr. Kidd, with a faint show of his old self-satisfied smile. " Our burgesses have rather utilitarian than æsthetic views."

" Like Mrs. Oscar," said Storker, " who would rather look upon a bit of striped grogram than on fifty emperor moths. Let us hope the connoisseurs will bid boldly. We must save all we can. When a man cuts his name on your table, you can at least gather up the chips."

"Oh, don't talk of a sale," pleaded Mrs. Kidd.

"I expect there must be a complete break-up," said Storker, grimly. "To judge from my father's countenance and words, I am afraid you might as well try to keep a decayed house together by repapering the walls, as to patch up his affairs with such money as he is likely to be able to scrape up."

"Perhaps he is only frightened and upset by the disappointment about papa," said Mrs. Kidd; "and time will make all well."

"There are certain liabilities I ought to clear off—but cannot," said Mr. Kidd.

"The people will wait," said she; "you will promise to pay them all you owe them— not that I wish to interfere."

"Who will join in such a guarantee?" he asked.

"Why need any one join in it. You are an honourable man, and the most interested in paying."

" It is not a question of will, but of power," said Storker, drily, "and my father, I am afraid, could pay about as easily as you could eat a brickbat buttered with tar."

" I feel almost as if I were standing on my head," said poor Mrs. Kidd. " My life won't be a long one, though a Howsegoe. Oh, why does this trouble come upon me ?"

" Why, indeed ?" said Storker.

" I shall never be so pleased to recognise the Howsegoe look in you again," said Mrs. Kidd, " though proud of the name I still am and must be—who is to blame me ? It's very sad my poor papa should have disappointed us all so much—I must say that—after all the trouble he has given us with his stews and egg-flip, and so on, his habit of standing be-fore the fire and wanting the best chair, and the best place on the pavement when walking; and, as to his temper at breakfast sometimes, it was very trying. But I shall never be full of days myself, and it's not for me to speak against the dead ; not that I believe in ghosts, though Betsy Briggs declares she saw her mother's ghost against the pump, but couldn't hear her words, which perhaps were not very pleasant, for she was in a sad passion just before she died, having had some young ducks with stubborn stumps sent her to pluck, and being too feeble to do the work."

" I suppose a good many people who can ill afford to lose their money are among your customers—and therefore creditors—father ?" said Storker.

" I fear so indeed," said Mr. Kidd ; " and one of the most distressing cases will be that of poor Boulder, whose entire treasure has been deposited with me."

"Ah, that is sad!" said Storker. "What will the young upstart Hern do now?"

"I can't tell. To be candid, I dare hardly think of that, or of the results of this misfortune of mine to many others. I am a little uncertain as to my exact position, but if the state of my affairs prove to be thoroughly bad, I will give up everything. My creditors shall have my coat and waistcoat if they wish, only I should be thankful for a few woollens if they turn me into the wilderness."

"Thankful!" cried Storker; "that is a very inappropriate word, but it would take a heavy blow to make you inclined to 'curse God and die.' For my part, I don't care to hear a man who has fallen down and broken his ribs chuckling that he didn't lose his watch-key."

"Don't flatter yourself that this calamity is not very bitter to me," said Mr. Kidd. "Only consider my tendency to generosity, and you'll allow that the loss of the power to encourage that tendency is in itself a punishment."

" It is odd you should calmly refer to one of your weaknesses," said Storker, testily, " in the face of a disaster to which it has contributed. But you were always as calm amid exciting circumstances as the riding lady in the circus-bills. You would fall to thinking and dreaming about the structure of your bedstead, though convinced that there was a burglar under it."

" I am at least glad that he has given you a good education and a profession in time, Storker," said his mother ; "not that I wish to blame your father in any way. He was always kind."

" I have no complaint to make of his lack of kindness to me," said Storker, warmly. " He would have given me, if he could have got it, a slice of the great wall of China, or some other strange thing about as useful to me as a boat to a bird of passage."

" I am especially sorry that things have turned out so badly, for your sake, Storker," said Mr. Kidd ; " but, hereafter, when I am out of business, I shall not again disappoint you."

" In other words, you break a man's back, sir, and promise not to do it again," said Storker, with a passing smile. " However, I am at least glad that you are going out of business, for it is clear to me that the less business you do the less money you will lose. While you are in business you will keep muddling about as restlessly as an old creaking gate on a breezy night. And as to farming, except on a very small scale, I should think you would give up the idea. You will have to content yourself with an occupation like that of Farmer Borley's, who goes to market in duffel gaiters, and says, ' chaw ' instead of

' masticate.' Perhaps you could earn a trifle in some other way, though I don't know what, unless you cut off your beard and sell it for an oil or a bannister brush."

" If I did that, my bald pate, with the aid of a frock and beads, would enable me to pass as a monk," said Mr. Kidd. " Well, well, without relinquishing my title to the possession of considerable business capacity, I confess I shall be glad to escape from the bank. I was never quite at my ease there, though one might think the routine not uncongenial to a man of uncommon mathematical talent."

" The mathematical talent was a nuisance and an intermeddler, I expect," said Storker. " When you should have been writing sharply to overdrawing customers, you were very likely calculating how many threads would be required to drag a dead elephant round the world."

" Ay, ay, but I am often practical with my

mathematical talent," said Mr. Kidd, with
strange complacency. "Few can tell you
more promptly the measurement of a stack or
a manure-heap, or the number of cubic feet of
digging in a drain or a railway-cutting, or the
contents of a bing of broken road-metal. I
could puzzle you, Storker, by asking you to
find the diameter of duodecagon, or the solidity
of an elliptic spindle. What do you know
about trone pounds?"

"As much as I want to know," said Storker,
coolly.

"I should think it's better to know about
golden pounds," said Mrs. Kidd, sadly, "and
how to take care of them."

"Well," said Mr. Kidd, "I have certainly
circulated a good many pounds. There has
been no 'laying by in a napkin' in my case.
But, though I may not have invested my
money prudently, I am by no means ignorant
of the money market, and I venture to think

few could give you better advice as to the best home and foreign mines; for I have drawn out statistics as to the sales of ore from many of them, with particulars of the quality of their plant and the amount of their working expenses."

" Oh, this talk seems all vain and useless," said Mrs. Kidd, " and it can't cure the trouble staring at us. Poor papa's death made us give up our dinner-party ; and now there is a worse mishap to keep Storker from Clara, and he may lose her for ever !"

" If I do," said Storker doggedly, but turning away his face, " ' perhaps I shall be the better for the loss,' as the woman said when her husband knocked a bad tooth down her throat."

" She's a good girl," said Mrs. Kidd, " though she has been so silly with this young Hern, who is worse bred than any tradesman's assistant in the town. Your father says he is very conservative on the subject of George Hern. For my part, I am not at all fond of the Radicals. Poor papa used to say they are generally 'the unripe in years and the rotten in fortune.' "

" We must hear what Oscar and his wife say," said Mr. Kidd, rising, "for we must at least keep on good terms with them, for Storker's sake."

" Oh, won't Mary Ann stare at us !" said Mrs. Kidd.

" Yes," said Storker, "and the town-clerk will speak to the point for once, I guess, instead of wandering from dish-clouts to clustered stars. But this is not the time to refer to his failings. Let us get dinner over, and then you can take the first important step by calling on the town-clerk and his lady—a merry excursion !"

With these words he left the room abruptly, almost pushing against · the smiling Bilge,

who had been stooping outside the door, with
his ear at the key-hole.

Shortly afterwards Storker once more
looked out thoughtfully from his dressing-
room window at the sea. The scene was
as fair as on the evening of his return, and
the picture of Clara Ashbocking was again
brought before his mind by it.

" My interest in you has increased, young
lady," he muttered, " while my hopes of securing you are lessened. Boulder's loss may
be one point in my favour, though I don't
like the thought, as my father is the cause.
Well, if I lose you, I must find comfort elsewhere, and hope for better days. Still, a
bird in the hand, etc., as the wolf said when
he stopped to devour his bulletted brother
rather than follow the sledge."

CHAPTER IX.

ON hearing from the banker the grim account
of his pecuniary collapse, the town-clerk
and his alert and prudent wife were filled
with astonishment and genuine dismay. The
unsuspected discovery of the Admiral's
poverty had stirred them very unpleasantly,
but they had not foreseen its effects upon the
good old business of Mr. Kidd Ashbocking.
Mrs. Oscar's face, which was of a dusky pale
hue when they entered the blue drawing-
room, darkened ominously during Mr. Kidd's
opening remarks, and she seemed to gasp for
breath more than once. When he had told
his unwelcome story, she left the room with-

out speaking. As she passed her husband, he recommended fortitude, and, in a muttered tone, quoted a fragment of Archilochus.

" But what are we to do ?" he said, turning with a clouded brow to his guests. " I can hardly guess. I dare form no decision at present. I intended to have had an hour at the Sardican Canons this evening, but this miserable announcement has driven them out of my mind, you may be sure. Bless my heart ! I am much hurt—as you perceive is my wife. Her countenance and her sudden withdrawal should be as expressive to you as another's railings and rantings."

Mrs. Oscar was absent but a few moments, but on her return she really looked as if she had been weeping. When she had resumed her customary chair, Mr. Kidd produced the statement of affairs prepared by himself and Storker, and Mr. Oscar read it aloud to his attentive wife.

"Founded partly on memory or conjecture, though this may be, it shows a bad estate," he exclaimed, looking up from the last item.

"A revelation," said Mrs. Oscar, harshly, "of ill-considered schemes, neglected duty, and ridiculous expenditure. Oscar, you and I have had a disagreement recently, and I have felt tempted to agree with this gentleman in thinking slightingly of your readings and talkings. But I return to your side this moment!"

"Thank you," said her husband; "Kidd has jeered at me for expressing regret that the world has but an imperfect knowledge of the opinion of Euripides on the merits of Homer——"

"One man's faults do not excuse another's weaknesses," said Mr. Kidd, mildly.

"Let me say at once and emphatically,"

said Mrs. Oscar, "that you ought to have let us know long ago the state of your affairs. I almost consider you wanting in fidelity."

" No, we won't say that," interposed Mr. Oscar. " If a Bedouin Sheikh eats with you, Niebuhr tells us, you may trust to his fidelity; we must at least expect as much from a respectable Englishman."

" Yours are hard words, Mary Ann," said Mr. Kidd, drawing a deep breath before he spoke. " To one who had only good intentions, yours are hard words. I hardly knew how far I had drifted to leeward, as they say; and yet," he added, musingly, " few men, I should think, have had more unpleasant experience of the speed with which time flies towards a payment-out, and the tardiness with which it crawls towards a payment-in."

" You have, indeed, drifted far to leeward," said the town-clerk. " You have, as Fuller says of Raleigh, 'run into day, and cannot creep out of it.'"

"It's dreadful to me, an ailing person," said Mrs. Kidd, wailingly; "not but what you look sadly enough, too, Mary Ann. But let us hope it's all for the best."

"If my opinion is worth anything, that's a queer hope," said Mrs. Oscar, impatiently.

"And yet possessing a philosophical flavour," said Mr. Oscar.

"I altogether object to such philosophy," retorted his wife. "What had you in the bank, pray?"

"A very small balance on my current account," said the town-clerk, in a tone of satisfaction. "I have always acted in accordance with your wishes in keeping my balance small."

"For scandal I care little," said Mrs. Oscar; "I think my mind is strong enough to surmount this: but the disgrace of insolvency is a disgrace indeed. Kidd, what on earth have you been doing ?"

" I must say I think my poor papa is very much to blame," exclaimed Mrs. Kidd, " in disappointing Kidd so terribly—not to mention Storker. Oh, what will Lady Stowers and Mrs. Monument and Mrs. Pittock say ?"

" Excuse the remark," said Mrs. Oscar; " but, you see, I was not altogether wrong in my rather poor opinion of the Admiral. He did not even deserve the praises I felt inclined to give him for the care he seemed to take of his money. He was a mulish man."

" I should imagine he was one who soon pushed himself from the questioning to the asserting age," said Mr. Oscar.

" Oh, yes," said Mrs. Kidd. " God forbid that I should speak against him, but, when he was quite a child, I have heard he had a terrible argument with my grandfather. He would have it that more stuff would grow on the slope of a hill than on the ground covered by its base, and my grandfather pushed him out of the room. Poor papa! his death was very sudden ; but he used to wear such tight things, I sometimes wondered he did not die of hysteric strangulation ; and just latterly, he drank very freely."

"So you thought he might die, like Hephæstion, of a fever brought on by drink ?" said Mr. Oscar. "The wound in the head, though, justifies us rather in comparing him to Scipio."

"His end was not very romantic," said Mrs. Oscar, "dying on the sofa after dinner."

"It does not much matter where one dies," said Mr. Kidd, thinking that the stern tones of the last speaker would hurt the feelings of his wife.

" That," said Mr. Oscar, "was the opinion
at the Sheikh Saadi."

" And now for *your* opinion upon Kidd's
affairs," said his wife.

" Yes, I have come for that," said Mr.
Kidd, " bringing my statement with me like
a rod, as it were, for my own chastisement.
Mere lamentation is vain ; we shall gain
nothing by fretting ourselves till we are as
pale as vitriol-bottlers."

" Your calmness is rather surprising," said
Mrs. Oscar, eyeing him.

" It always was," said Mrs. Kidd. "When
poor papa was in one of his passions, sometimes Kidd would quietly touch the weather-
glass, and say, ' I'm afraid a storm is gather-
ing,' and his smile would make the Admiral
cool down ; and, perhaps, it is best to be
cool, and say, ' all for the best.' "

" I would as soon hear a person say, ' I
can't help it,' and despair, as ' All for the

best,' and smile !" cried Mrs. Oscar, angrily. " I feel disgusted !" she added, rising impulsively and adjusting a chair against the wall. " I wish to exercise the restraint due to prudence and womanly propriety, but to-night, I confess, I feel sick of my life, and almost believe I am growing crazy."

" No, no, my dear," said Mr. Oscar, soothingly. " I know few people for whom the fate of Cleomenes could be predicted with less reason."

Mrs. Oscar sat down again and smoothed her dress, but her face was stern and disturbed.

" I am not proud," she said, in a hard tone. " I should have no objection to carrying a bag of flour or a bonnet-box through the streets. I am not ashamed to have it known that I make my own felt carpets, and many other things, or that I do much work in the kitchen, and have used a bottle for a rolling-pin more than once : but I feel humi-miliated by this mishap of Kidd's; I do, indeed. I would almost as willingly have given up Oscar's manors of Pigham-with-the-members and Broom-Blackness as have it known throughout the country that his cousin is insolvent !"

" A proud man of power once made a little MS. note—' Pride made angels devils' "—said Mr. Oscar; " but I must think your pride, Mary Ann, a worthy and excusable one."

" No doubt all the prosperous will say that," said Mrs. Kidd, with a sigh. " Storker says the world will very soon be making a whisper about us, like the whirring of a flock of sparrows. But I hope you won't turn against us."

" I hope not," said Mrs. Oscar, sharply; " but Kidd ought to know that a man who is his own enemy is likely to thin the ranks of his friends one day."

"I regret the disgrace ; but I hope I shall be able, in the future, to make up to you any pecuniary loss you may sustain through me," said Mr. Kidd, gently, "though the amount, indeed, must seem small to you—the owners of Ashbocking Street."

"Perhaps so," said Mrs. Oscar, frowning at him; "yet as we have never been speculators, we have not destroyed our taste for small gains. But, as to future repayment, it's easier to lay hands on the property of a foreign government than on the 'no property' of an insolvent after his affairs are wound up. I therefore propose that, as a first step, you deliver up to us a few articles of value to cover our loss."

"We have nothing here, I fear," said Mr. Kidd, "unless you strip Bella of her plumage. I have little about me beside a silver watch, a screw belonging to a mangle, a bit of pump-leather, a cork, and a florin."

"Don't talk idly ; I don't allude to what you have here," was Mrs. Oscar's rejoinder. "But as you refer to Bella's plumage, make a note of and bring us a few such items as these—Bella's dress of blue popline, with the shell trimming, the electric blue sash, the white venetian scarf, the coiffure with red velvet rosettes, and the robe of Indian green silk, with under sleeves of Honiton lace. These things may be adapted and toned down for Clara one day, perhaps ; and, though we must make a considerable deduction from their cost price, are of some value."

"Oh, I don't like the idea of impoverishing my stock of dresses or anything else at Castle House," cried Mrs. Kidd. "Shall I have to give up my good old Spanish point-lace and my Mechlin pillow-lace borders?"

"I don't wish to speak harshly to you, Arabella," said Mrs. Oscar, turning upon her.

" No, no," said the town-clerk, hastily. " It is easy to be a Zoilus—an illiberal critic, Mary Ann, and that is sometimes worse than being a Bellanger—an incompetent one.

" Well, think of the items I have mentioned," said Mrs. Oscar, " and let us come to the point as to what else is to be done."

" The assets are so discouraging," said the town-clerk, shaking his head, " that I must take time to consider what advice I shall offer. I am glad to see that there is about a pipe of Dingall's port, and a tolerable stock of other wines. Then there is your diamond, which is almost fit for a state diadem. As to your books, I know they are but a poor collection. I think that ' Romaine's Discourses,' ' Strype's Memorials,' and the ' Jubar Astrologicum ' are the only volumes of which I have not copies."

" You must leave me one or two favourite

books," said Mr. Kidd, in a subdued voice, "such as my 'Davis on Land Surveying,' and my 'Keay's Tables for Timber Mensuration.' You are quite welcome to my 'Stuckey on Country Banking.' I should also like to retain the carved oak napkin-press, which I partly made with my own hands, and my pocket clinometer."

"And the stool embroidered by me," said Mrs. Kidd, "and the Dresden porcelain chocolate cups that Major Dobbs gave me, and——"

"If you go on in that way," said Mrs. Oscar, sternly, "you will leave your creditors a set of unmarketable gimcracks, some clothes of yours, Bella—too smart for people of taste to wear—and some of Kidd's, only fit to burn."

"Certainly, Kidd's garments are not like those of Lucullus," said Mr. Oscar.

"But my curiosities, pictures, and sculptures, if properly dealt with, are of not a little value," said Mr. Kidd. "They will, however, require great care, taste and judgment in valuation—if such a course is found to be necessary."

"I might help you somewhat there," said Mr. Oscar. "I can look up 'Pilkington's Dictionary,' 'Cellini's Autobiography'——"

"Pray don't talk about the curiosities," said Mrs. Oscar, in a tone of disgust. "They have been in a great measure the cause of Kidd's making such a poor figure."

"Still they evince good taste," said Mr. Kidd, mildly.

"Good taste doesn't make great men," said Mrs. Oscar, scornfully.

"Nor does money make men wholly and fully great," said Mr. Kidd, "even if it be a Nabob's fortune."

"No, nor yet meanness," said Mrs. Kidd; "not that I wish to hurt your feelings or call you mean, Mary Ann; but you must not trample too much on us. If we had been mean, we shouldn't have been here in this plight, ready to be trampled on. But meanness makes nobody great, for Oscar quoted a wise man's saying the other day, which was something like this : 'Nothing is great the contempt of which is great,' and I'm sure my contempt for meanness is very great."

"If you judge merit from a monetary and fiscal stand-point only, Mary Ann," said the banker, "of course I am contemptible in your eyes.'

"I am not at all influenced by your opinions, but I don't deny certain merits to you," she replied curtly. "You can do many things—can tell, for instance, how the sun and moon act on the winds, and whether a coat has much cotton in it. It's a pity, as to your own coat, by-the-by, that you don't ascertain how much dust is in it; and as to your boots, I should often feel ashamed to show them to the cleaner. But we are wandering from the point. I don't wish to castigate you. The public will do that, and the fact that you deserve their censure is painful to me, for my husband's interest is so closely bound up with that of the public of this neighbourhood, that you can't harm the one without the other."

" The public will show me some conside-ration, I think," said Mr. Kidd.

" I fear there will be not a little disap-probation expressed," said Mr. Oscar. " For even those who lose nothing will be disap-pointed, as you have been thought to be one of those popular favourites—a man of wealth and power who can be mild-mannered and easy-going, nevertheless."

"You must, of course, expect a little hard treatment," said Mrs. Oscar.

"But for the sake of our old friendship, I hope you won't be hard upon us, Mary Ann," said the banker. "You must remember that loyalty and slavery are not more inconsistent than harshness and good-will."

"You should not have placed yourself in a position enabling me to deal harshly with you," replied Mrs. Oscar, coolly.

"I should have acted more frequently upon your favourite maxims, such as 'Look out for Number One,' and 'Get value received,'" said Mr. Kidd.

"And very sensible and useful maxims they are," said Mr. Oscar. "Remember Bacon's words : 'Why should I be angry with a man for loving himself better than me?' Mary Ann once took a fancy to another maxim also, a legal one, viz., 'Nothing is more just than what is necessary,' and this she applies to me in urging me to the acquisition of costs, which, she says with truth, is a very necessary proceeding. Hume has told us that nothing has a greater tendency to give us esteem for any person than his power and riches; and, though Syrus has held that God looks only to pure and not to full hands, we none of us think the worse of Joseph of Arimathæa on account of his wealth."

"Mary Ann was always fond of picking up a little," said Mrs. Kidd. "When she was a school-girl, I have heard, she would write home pretty regularly for supplies. And she was always a careful one, and would inquire into the contents of a covered dish very soon after its appearance at table."

"I have found care of service to me in passing through life," said Mrs. Oscar, with quiet scorn, "and therefore I still endeavour to be careful. Nor do I think you can find

me a substitute for care. I certainly decline
to accept your dinner-wine bills as such."

" I believe," said Mr. Kidd, with a melancholy smile, "that if you paid your creditors
a dividend of a farthing in the pound, and
heard that there was a surplus of twopence-
halfpenny in the hands of your solicitor, you
would call upon him for it."

" And I believe," she retorted, sharply,
" that if you called upon a creditor to arrange
to pay him a farthing in the pound, you
would give his servant half-a-crown for hand-
ing you your hat."

" Oh, pray let us have no quarrelling,"
said Mrs. Kidd. " Angry words send a
shiver down my back. Besides, we have
trouble enough before us now."

" Yes, we should remember that," said Mr.
Oscar, kindly, " though however small one's
trouble, one's neighbours are apt to esteem it
smaller still."

"I didn't intend to hurt your feelings, Mary Ann," said Mr. Kidd, always ready for peace. "I am not angry," he added, rather ruefully.

"Mary Ann is aware of that, Kidd," said Mr. Oscar; "and really, considering the great trouble that must be preying upon your mind, I rather admire your calmness."

"Will it get him a meal, or clothes, or a new cheval-glass if his favourite one is sold?" asked Mrs. Oscar, sharply.

"I think you are too severe on my want of prudence and economy," said Mr. Kidd, with another melancholy smile; "if these virtues are exercised to excess——"

"Thank you, Kidd," said Mrs. Oscar, with a cold sarcastic nod. "The Sunday sermons supply all my ethical needs."

"I am sure Kidd doesn't wish to preach you any sermons," said Mrs. Kidd, "for he's not fond of them. And I'm sure I don't

wish to either. I shall want some clergy-
men's comfort myself, and some doctors' too."

"You have had few real troubles before,
my friend," said Mrs. Oscar, "but you could
not expect to live your time in the world
without a taste or two of bitterness ; for it
abounds in it."

"Ay," said Mr. Oscar, "and some live
daily under a sword, like Damocles. But
hard experience in the case of all, as in that
of Virgil, enables us the better to sympathise
with the suffering."

"It's very hard," said Mrs. Kidd, "but I
don't wish to interfere or to grumble. I
shall try to be contented with woes and
grievances, and to give up willingly what
makes life bright and comfortable. I had an
idea that farming corn-fields, except as an
amusement, would be a degradation. I had an
idea that things would be very different, but
I must give that up."

" Well said !" exclaimed Mr. Oscar. "Some
people would rather cast out a parent on his
sinking into dotage than an idea on its
lapsing into absurdity. Depend upon it,
Bella, sorrow is as necessary to the soul as
night to the earth."

" I don't think I have made luxuries and
superfluities altogether essential to my hap-
piness," said Mrs. Kidd. " Golden embroidery doesn't make a person happy
within. I don't think mine will be a long
life, though the Howsegoes have generally
been strong. I think I can reconcile myself
to part with some of my dresses (and, after
all, dressing is a great nuisance) and some of
my jewellery, if it must go : and, indeed, it
may be best to let it go. Poor Mark
Magub the sailor had a ring which he was
very fond of, but it was no great friend to
him, for one day when he was clambering

about his ship, it caught in something and pulled his finger out of the socket."

" The concession of your decorations will be a brave and a worthy one," said Mr. Oscar, "for you have jewellery which would adorn you as gorgeously as the lady in the ballad of ' Young Bateman,' not to mention silks which would not be scorned by a nobleman of Turkestan, and furs which would have brought you into disrepute in the days of the Statute of Apparel."

" And what about the possibility of your having to work, Bella ?" asked Mrs. Oscar sneeringly.

" That is even more unpleasant," replied the lady of Castle House, " for I expected to have less of this as time went on, although Kidd sometimes used to say I might have to do some of the work of a dairy-maid. At other times he would say I might lie in bed till the scent of the dinner roused me. I suppose men think it proper to talk nonsense to women sometimes, because, as Storker says, women will tack their fringe of nonsense to men's plain words. But as to men and women, especially in the matter of gardening, I believe that men do as much harm by interfering with women's work as women do by interfering with men's. By the way, I hope we shall be able to keep poor dear Ariel, though he won't like to leave Castle House, even if we do, for he can't bear to be put out of a place he has been in the habit of frequenting, though only for a short time every day."

"No doubt he could go with you," said Mr. Oscar, kindly, "unless, indeed, you are reduced to living in the fashion of George Mangle, mentioned in an old law case, who had half a bed at one and sixpence per week."

"I hope we shan't come to that," said

Mrs. Kidd, looking at her husband, " or so that we shall have to use a bit of ˙waggon-tilt for a coverlet, and an old towel for a window-blind instead of one of bobbin and book-muslin—not that I want a room hung with crimson brocade. I dare say I could live on bread and cheese with a herring-pie or a fig-pudding for a treat. I can even think it possible that I could work in the rag-room of a shoddy-mill, if I might have a clean little nook for my meals and bed ; though when the bare floors were too cold to stand on, I might try to do my toilet on the bed in the dark (for of course we could not afford a candle) and lose my balance and tumble into the bath. But I don't wish to interfere—what say you, Kidd ?"

" I shall part, with sincere regret, from many things I possess," said Mr. Kidd, taking off his spectacles to wipe them ; " but I am ready to face my new position. In a lowered station I shall at least be more free from the miserable constraints and pretences of Society, and can look at things from a more independent stand-point, which means, a wiser and a worthier one. Poverty has its charm."

" As Juvenal says," exclaimed Mr. Oscar, "'the man with an empty pocket can sing before the robber.'"

" I have no wish to die, nor would I speak imprudently," interposed Mrs. Oscar, very sternly ; "but if I were Kidd, I could hardly survive the degradation which he talks about so coolly."

" I have no intention of entering yet upon 'death's dateless night,' I assure you, Mary Ann," said Mr. Kidd.

"Why, you are in the prime of life," said Mr. Oscar ; " Agesilaus at eighty undertook a distant expedition in the pay of a foreign power."

"I can yet earn an honest living," said Mr. Kidd, "even if I have to wear tow-cloth, like Chaucer's shipman. I can work as an architect or a master-builder. I am well acquainted with aquatic and marine mysteries. I have looked at the sea carefully almost every day for many years. I can make a bargain. I can at least sell matches or india-rubber rings, or tomato-sauce or elderberry-and-wort-wine made from my favourite re-cipes. I can keep a pig, and kill him at rent-time, as our Suffolk cottagers do."

"Or you can dwindle into an imbecile pauper," said Mrs. Oscar, "and give away towns in your dreams. I am tired of this conversation. I am extremely jealous of Oscar's reputation, but I shall try to comfort myself by thinking that your disgrace is not his, and I shall not hold my head an inch lower on account of it. You and he are distinct persons, thank God."

"If men were made in duplicate and tri-
plicate," said Mr. Oscar, "there would be
fewer volumes of philosophy."

"Oh dear, dear," exclaimed Mrs. Kidd.
"And are we so utterly disgraced. And
there is the annual meeting of our branch
of the London City Mission just at hand
(a good society, for rough wicked English-
men are as bad as savages, and I have a
horror of both of them), and next Sunday we
preach sermons for the Propagation people;
and Mrs. Mudd was saying that our Dorcas
clothes are somewhat deficient, so that a
special meeting would be advisable, and she
proposed to hold one at Castle House."

"It was the best place—at one time," said
Mrs. Oscar, drily. "Your tea-table was
tempting, and would draw a good company
of the pious—a sort of fish you can always
catch if you bait with creature-comforts."

"But, now, before we go," said Mrs. Kidd,

"what about the worst of all—what about poor Storker ?"

" He had better try to marry some rich widow," said Mrs. Oscar, shortly.

" Like Apuleius," said her husband. " I should recommend him to devote himself seriously to business, and to act upon the apopthegm of Ichomachus——"

Mrs. Oscar stopped her husband by an expressive cough.

Mrs. Kidd paused for a moment, and then said, hesitatingly :

" May he not yet take his chance with Clara ?"

" I have always thought his chance a hope-less one," said the town-clerk, with unusual firmness.

" Clara is no common girl, and I'm afraid your son has not tastes similar to her own," said Mrs. Oscar, " or to mine. He has too much of the Howsegoe dandyism about him."

"I am not going to quarrel with my son for the sake of a broadcloth coat or a pair of doeskin trousers," said Mrs. Kidd.

"Let us for the present drop this subject," said Mr. Oscar. "Perhaps Storker is to be congratulated that no one is likely to urge him on in this love-affair just now. The fickle god is a troublesome personage, and Bion tells us how the old man congratulated the Fowler on being free from him. At the same time, I think that every one should be able to repeat with pleasure Richter's dictum, 'It is with emotion and good wishes that I witness the caresses of two virtuous lovers.'"

"I trust Storker will settle well and be happy," said Mrs. Kidd, rather heavily. "I might have been an old maid, but when I was a girl, though in some things considered to be as green as a young gooseberry, I looked out and soon found a husband, and a good one in many respects no doubt, if not in a pecuniary point of view. But, talking of Clara, what about Boulder's money and George Hern ?"

" I have several times thought of that during this evening," said Mr. Oscar; " and I shall give it my serious consideration, as well as your own position."

Mrs. Oscar shuffled her feet impatiently, and the disconsolate visitors rose to depart.

END OF VOL. II.

BILLING AND SONS, PRINTERS, GUILDFORD, SURREY.